A Rogue
A Pirate
and
A Dry Martini

This book is a work of fiction. All names, places, characters and events
described herein are the products of the author's imagination and are used
fictiously. Any resemblance to actual persons living or dead, events or locales
is entirely coincidental.

FOR MY ONE
AND ONLY
THOMAS
O'ROURKE

Chapter One

RIP *Morgan Sidney*, the laughing girl private eye. Well, that's TV, the junk heap of shattered dreams. I liked playing Morgan. Millions of Americans liked Morgan. But after five years of laughing her way out of trouble, the ratings dropped and it's asta la vista, baby. Hey it was fun while it lasted.

Am I disappointed? You bet your full frontal nude shot I am. There I was with a nice clean series, no pissing scenes, no bathroom scenes, no having to commit unspeakably personal acts with perfect strangers for public consumption. Not even a little titty or some bare ass every now and then. None of that shit. No, all Morgan had to do was solve a crime every week, and do some laughing, often when she was really in trouble. It was an oddly believable quirk. Laughter wells up from the most primitive part of the brain. There's something curiously anarchic, disconcerting, and even rebellious about laughter. It always caught the criminals and cops off guard, threw them off their game, worked like a charm, just as long as you didn't overdo it. And it wasn't as easy as it sounds. You can't fake real laughter. The mirthless guffaw of the politician is proof of that.

Really, it's almost cruel to turn someone into a Hollywood star. Your whole life becomes about the money. Since the beginning of time, everyone who has more money, or slaves, or camels than someone else, assumes they are superior—they become the aristocracy, or the priest king, or the Warren Buffet of the world. And everyone assumes that the rich are rich because they *are* better, finer, smarter, and sexier than anyone else on the planet. People with money encourage this erroneous illusion, and often fall for it themselves; in Hollywood it's called believing your own publicity. But everyone who makes it out here in Hollyweird, even for fifteen minutes, has so much money, at some point in their careers, that they could rake thousand dollar bills off their lawn and burn them. Stars enjoy being looked up to like they're Gods. And for heaven's sake, it costs a bundle to keep *that* illusion going: wrinkle free face, non-cellulite thighs, perfect teeth, non-droop tits, great hair. WOW! How do you afford that?

So there you are, you poor star; rich, popular and getting lots of attention. Clearly everyone wants to be like you, if only you'll tell them how. And you begin to ponder endlessly this monumentally wonderful question—it's your second favorite question after what will I say when I win my Oscar—'oh how did I get to be marvelous me?' It's cruel. All alone up there on a pedestal and nothing to think about but how did I get to be so?... So? Wonderful? Gorgeous? Brilliant? But most of us never add that last most revealing word until the pedestal is shattered, like me, today. So lucky? Yeah, that's really a big part of what got you there. Dumb luck. Worked for me. But, hey, the food was great. Picasso on a plate and tasting just like you always knew Picasso should taste.

Well, Bernie my agent will find something for me. There's gotta be life after a long running TV series. SOMETHING! If only I could get to Bernie's office. Instead, I'm sitting in the Hollywood Hills traffic on my way to the Valley where my studio is, and I'm fuming amid the fumes of the morning rush hour. So what else is new in LA? I'm stuck in the daily convoy of Mercedes, Jags, and Hummers, or, in my case, a vintage Mustang convertible, all creeping toward the Promised Land in hopes of snagging something big that will enable us to actually afford these fancy cars and extravagant lifestyles so dear to our greedy little hearts.

We snake back and forth, one hair pin turn after another, up through Beverly Glen, across the Santa Monica Mountains, past some of the most expensive real estate in the world. You'd think at the price this land goes for that it would be breathtakingly beautiful, but no, it's just one lumpy dirt hill after another, haphazardly overgrown with brush and scrub so ugly and thorny the military could use the stuff as an anti-personal weapon. The Hollywood Hills are about as attractive as a five mile long raw construction site. The roadside, which we all have ample time to study in detail, is littered with rocks and clods of dirt that have tumbled down from the overhanging, overpriced homes perched above the road—until the next mudslide sends a mansion or two careening down with all the other unattractive rubble.

Ahead of me, the valley stretches out for miles in the hazy distance to the imposing Santa Clarita Mountains, which have actually grown a couple of inches taller due to earthquakes since I've been here. Little streets and homes laid out in postage stamp size lots are shimmering in the morning sun and smog. It's February and only nine am, but the sun is already fierce in the unrelenting blue sky. Well, at least I've got plenty of time to reflect on what the hell I'm doing in this business and where I want to get personally, my life goals, etc., and the always interesting and terrifying monthly challenge—how am I going to pay my mortgage?

What can Bernie do for me? Nothing and everything. Just get me the chance to meet the people with the jobs. He's old Hollywood and knows where all the skeletons are buried. Plus, he's got leverage in the form of several highly sought after clients, including me.

Technically, I'm an actress. These days, for some reason, there are no actresses in Hollywood, only actors. The actress word has fallen out of favor. Feminists, in the name of women's liberation, have eliminated the feminine form of the noun—go figure. It's as if everyone out here in LA is trying to pretend actors and actresses are interchangeable. Like 'we're looking for an actor to play Scarlett O'Hara'. Right. How about Johnny Depp? Does that work for you? Johnny is certainly the prettiest actor in Hollywood, and he wore eye make-up in the *Pirates of the Caribbean*. Will he do? So where does that leave me? Can the former Morgan Sidney become the new Magnum PI? Do I need a hairy chest for that role?

How did I ever get mixed up in the crazy business? Oh wait! I remember. It was my dear old stage mom. The bored Valley housewife, who always dreamed of being a movie star, but the trials and tribulations of actually *working* were not her style. She'd done her bit by having me. So, at age three, I was elected to fulfill her gassy ambitions and help pay the bills, when dear old Dad took a powder. Not that I blame him, only a masochist would have stayed with her once the thrill of young love had worn off. The child support check, in my mother's twisted logic, conveniently became the check to help the child support herself and the mother she needed to take care of her. We would never starve, but it was the blood, sweat and tears of my childish brow that provided our little luxuries, like manicures and fast food.

It's going to be quite a blow to her bragging rights that I'm not a regular on TV anymore. She'll be calling me every day, telling me all the parts I should be up for and wondering incessantly in that subtly undermining way of hers why I'm not a bigger star, by now. She'll do whatever it takes to goad and badger me on to greater fame and celebrity. Wonderful.

But, in spite of what Mom thinks, I've done okay. Even though I'm not exactly a household name, I do have money in the bank that will last me through a few tough years, if it has to, along with a steady diet of spaghetti.

With this happy thought, I finally drive out of the hills and down the last block on my way to Bernie's office, which is on the studio lot—my studio, or rather my former studio. The impregnable walled castle of movie production looms up bedside my Mustang, about five stories high. The studio enclave is surrounded by miles of pale stucco walls enclosing acres and acres of highly secret movie making. The walls are garishly decorated with enormous posters of upcoming film releases.

I'm heading for the main gate, where, if you are somebody, (and today, I'm still somebody) you get to drive onto the lot. The Mustang bumps along the yellowed, cracked old concrete street, as I guide it into the main gate. A cute little guardhouse sits between the in and out lanes. I imagine they must have had checkpoints like this along the Berlin Wall, minus the cascades of fuchsia bougainvillea, of course. The uniformed guard recognizes me easily enough in my convertible and waves me through.

The studio is an immense old complex of buildings and stages, a teeming bee hive of activity, with narrow little streets that have names like Daryl Zanuck Drive, running between the six story high, city block size, airplane hangar huge stages. Stages that are big enough, for instance, to accommodate the entire four story

Addams Family Victorian house and front yard, or a Busby Berkley fantasy dance stairway to Heaven, with extra room overhead for director, cameraman, camera, and God, with another forty feet or so for lighting grids, rigging, and cranes to move scenery flats easily and efficiently wherever they are needed. It's a sprawling factory devoted to the creation of illusion, and it does have its charms.

Like many of the studios out here, this one began its career in the nineteen twenties, when the sunlight was free, Thomas Edison and his motion picture legal patents too far away in New York to cause trouble, and the public hungry for the flickering black and white images of life as it might be, or as it all too often was. As the fortunes of my studio rose and fell, new offices and stages were built to house bigger and newer productions. This has lent a certain slapdash air to the layout of my home studio. In fact, some of the stages and offices are nightmares of hasty construction mistakes. There are hallways to nowhere, and little stairways to correct for different floor levels here and there as you walk from a Forties era office building with real windows that open, to a Fifties typing pool that looks like Ward Cleaver works there and on to a severely modern setting, all glass windows, and all hermetically sealed.

My Mustang is now creeping about five miles an hour down Busby Berkeley Drive through the seductively cool, jasmine and orange blossom scented air that makes spring mornings in the Valley so California dreamy. I'm stuck behind a guy on a bike with a handlebar basket full of scripts. He's probably a Harvard grad wondering when he'll make it out of the mailroom. But even if he pulled over, it would be a squeeze to slip by him. The road is only wide enough for the other usual mode of transportation, golf carts, to pass each other.

It's nine fifteen when I park in front of Bernie's office building. It's a quaint, two story bungalow on a little orange tree plaza, nestled between the big stage buildings, which he is privileged to use because of his family's old Hollywood connections. They've all been in this business since his grandfather left Brooklyn, way back when. Bernie has showed me old photos from those days. Riverside Boulevard, now a four-lane thoroughfare with shopping malls and gas stations, was just a dirt road through the orchards that lined the valley. He has several shots of his grandfather posing with the cowboys riding their horses down Riverside to report for work in the hundreds of Westerns they used to crank out at this studio back then.

My meeting is at nine thirty, which gives me fifteen minutes to make the call I've been dreading all morning. I light up a ciggie, suck up some smoke to relax, and grab the cell phone. (Technically, I've quit smoking, just not today.) It's gotta be done. Justin will wonder why I didn't call him earlier. We've been part of *Morgan Sidney* together from the beginning. He's my producer. I'm his star. I'm sure he's just as devastated as I am. Of course, it is somewhat easier for a producer to find work, than for a performer. But we're old friends. Well, really more than that. Sleeping together for the last five years—I guess that qualifies as more than friend. Truthfully, I was probably cast as Morgan Sidney because Justin was my boyfriend and pushed for me to get the role. Not that I hadn't 'paid my dues', that quaint Hollywood expression which means you've been offered a chance to sleep with everyone in Hollywood who might conceivably do your career some good, from the overweight casting woman who's never had a happy day in her life to just about anyone with some sort of genitals, but you had some pride and intelligence and didn't hop into bed with every single one of them; and so having stood emotionally and often physically naked and vulnerable before the Gorgons of show business, you've earned your spurs and gone on to work another day. However, I take pride in the fact that a five year run with great ratings proved his confidence in me was not simply a bad case of lust. I'm sure he'll be great about it. It wasn't my fault, just one of those things. Okay, face reality. Make the call.

"Hi Brandy...I'm fine...considering. How about you? Can I speak to Justin? (Pause for her executive secretary bullshit.) Brandy, gimme a break with that 'in a meeting' stuff, okay? You know why I'm calling. (On hold. Cold sweat. Hands shaking. Will he take my call?) Justin, Hi. Yeah, I just got the news this morning that they cancelled Morgan. Somebody saw it in Variety and called me. (Stomach acid churns) You had to read it in Variety, too? They didn't tell you either, huh? (Liar, liar, pants on fire.) I'm fine. I'm dealing with it. (He's getting very defensive. What's going on here?) Alright, maybe I am a little testy. Is that a big surprise? I'm unemployed for the first time in five years. I'm in total shock, but I'M DEALING WITH IT! (I'm dizzy and can't quite process whatever it is he's saying.) My shrink? Yes of course, I'm still seeing my shrink. But that doesn't mean I don't need a little love and support from my friends...and lovers. (Oh shit! I can't believe I said that. Pathetic. And I blunder on with a nervous laugh.) So, are we still on for dinner tonight? (I'm now officially groveling.) No, I don't understand why you *have* to go out with Melissa Jones. (He's a total heel.)

A Rogue, A Pirate, and A Dry Martini

Yes, I know you always said part of your job was romancing the talent. I just thought you meant it metaphorically. (I'm lighting another cigarette, and I *never* smoke before my evening cocktail.) Metaphorically? (What an idiot!) It means I never thought you were *literally* going to get in bed with the girl who got my time slot. Look, all these double entendres are getting me crazy, let's just...It doesn't matter what double entendre means! Where the hell are we in this relationship? (Like I care, you ignorant dip shit!) Sure, Yeah. Let's just let it ride. (That's producer lingo for I'll never take your call again.) I won't have much time anyway. I've got to concentrate on my career. I'm on my way to a meeting with Bernie right now. See you...Yeah, later."

That went well. I slap the phone shut, swearing like a sailor. Great. I need a minute to pull myself together. Since the only car parked under the orange trees in front of Bernie's office is mine, I assume he's running a little late. I lay back and stare up through the dark green waxy leaves at the sky and light up another cigarette. Damn Justin! Romancing the talent!!! I'm thirty. Is that too old to go on living? In Hollywood, that's way over the hill. I'm out of work. My *ex* boyfriend is dating the teenager who replaced me. I've never been married. Never been in love. Justin and I didn't even live together. We liked each other. That's all.

So what's so hard about losing a friend you occasionally had adequate sex with? Because now it's obvious we had nothing. It seemed like something, but it was nothing. I've wasted five years, and I'm thirty, and I'm nowhere. Shit.

Just another beautiful day in Hollywood. Can't they ever have a friggin cloudy day out here! What a relief a rainstorm would be about now: great big fat gray clouds, hovering low in the sky, portentous, melancholy, swelling with doom. It's so bizarre to sit here in endless summer on the worst day of my life. I'm so officially Hollywood brain dead.

I finish the cigarette, and zombie girl gets out of the car, enters the quaint office, and says hi to the receptionist. Bernie is running late, but I'm welcome to wait inside his office. Good. Bernie is like a surrogate parent, or a real parent, or something like that.

I plop down into a deep leather armchair. Suddenly, I can breathe again. I love Bernie's office. It's all cozy and warm and human size. So civilized. It has two walls of mullioned windows, each with outdoor flower boxes bursting with pink and white geraniums. The other two walls are lined with vintage Hollywood posters, Bernie's family treasures, complete with autographs: Flynn, De Havilland, Gable, Lombard, Powell, Loy, and Harlow—all the greats. What faces they had! Yeah, it's true, like in Sunset Boulevard, the stars were bigger then, it's the pictures that got small. I sigh, feeling sorry for myself and my entire generation of film history. Not all the steamy sex scenes or thrill ride car chases or mucous dripping aliens can ever banish these ghosts of Hollywood's truly glamorous past. Even their photographs seem to haunt Bernie's office, casting a spell over it.

God, I love that man. Bernie's sixty something, and a big guy, in that slightly hefty, character actor way. Salt and pepper gray hair, always tan, and always warm, sensible, full of good humor and shrewd advice. Bernie will make everything all right. He'll save my career. If anyone can do it, he can. Besides, we've always had a thing for each other, in a very father daughter way, of course.

With a few minutes to kill, I notice a breakdown sheet on Bernie's desk: a list of all the parts that are casting now in the movies and TV shows. Maybe if I just take a peek, it'll cheer me up.

Humm. Casting for a "pouty sex kitten" for a new evening soaper. "Brittany was a high priced hooker, but she's going to try to get some self respect. She's going back to school to study law so she can get into politics." Oh right. That's believable. Like lawyers and politicians are more respectable than hookers.

Hey, here's one. "Thirty year old career woman: so successful that she can't find a man who isn't intimidated by her, but has a warm loving relationship with her cat." I could do that. I intimidate all the men I meet, if you can call producers men.

The door behind me opens, and I turn to see Bernie's kind, sympathetic smile. He holds his arms out, and we embrace.

"Hey, kiddo, how're ya doing?"

He holds me just long enough to make me feel better and not so long that I collapse in tears.

"Bernie, I can't tell you how good it is to see you. I feel better already."

We sit down opposite each other, like doctor and patient.

"Well," I sniffle, "Morgan Sidney PI, is finally going to give up snooping. I knew it had to end someday, but I hate it."

"Hey, you had a great run. You've been careful with your money. You've got plenty to live on."

"Yeah, if I move to Peoria."

Marcy Casterline

"So? What's wrong with Peoria? Come on, the show will be on cable for years. That and DVD's will pay your bills. You'll be fine. If you're careful, you'll never have to work again. Being broke, that's the worst. Happens to a lot of performers. So sad. But not you kiddo!"

"I know, and I really appreciate everything you've done for me. Your investment people have been great. But what about my career? Where do I go now? It's time to grow up and be a leading lady, isn't it?"

"And you've never looked better. You've got style and intelligence, and you're a darn good actress. You're my favorite client, you know."

"Oh, Bernie, you make me feel almost hopeful."

Bernie sits back in his chair and folds his hands together, looking very serious.

"Kiddo, as your friend and advisor, my suggestion is... retire. Quit while you're ahead."

I'm dumbfounded. This is Bernie my agent telling me to *retire*! This is my second earthquake shock of a typical multi-faceted Hollywood day—cancelled *and* told to retire—kill me now. What's going on? I should have listened to my astrologer and gone on a long trip.

"Retire? But why? I'm still in my prime. You just said I looked great."

"I know, and I meant it. But the problem is there just isn't any work around for you."

"Why? I don't get it. Is it my age? Thirty isn't *that* old, is it?"

"Age isn't the problem, it's your type."

"But, I'm an actress. I can play lots of types."

"Yeah, but they're all the wrong types for what's on the screen today."

"What do you mean?" I'm totally flabbergasted. I can't be hearing this. Bernie is a show biz guru, a veteran. He's never wrong. "I don't get it?" I whimper helplessly.

He shifts in his chair and looks pained. "I'll try to explain. What kind of movies do they do a lot of these days? Well, for one, there are buddy pictures. You know, two guys always getting into lots of trouble: one dumb, one smart; one crazy, one normal; one has lots of girlfriends, the other is married or no one will date him. Lots of action, lostsa guns, karate, fist fights, dirty jokes. The girl is just window dressing."

I nod and roll my eyes. "I avoid seeing those movies whenever possible. So boring!"

"Men love them. For that kind of film, they want either a sexy girl, who eats, sleeps, and drinks sex, never has another thought but getting laid. Or the hometown, too-sweet-to-be-true girl. The trouble is you're neither."

"Okay, true. I'm too sophisticated to be the hometown girl, and I'm certainly not the horney bimbo sex object. But I could do it. I have a good figure."

"Doesn't matter. You look too smart. Put you opposite those studs, and you make them look stupid."

"They *are* stupid!" I point out in exasperation, not because Bernie doesn't already know this, but because I'm having a bad day that seems to be getting worse.

"Look, kiddo," Bernie advises, trying to calm me down. "We're talking about getting jobs here, not my opinion of the kind of shit that people in this town get all funny over. Even if you didn't have any lines, your eyes ask questions those idiots couldn't answer with their voices dubbed."

I sigh and sink back into my chair. He's right. I know he's right.

"Bernie, how about a women's picture? I'd be happy to do a TV movie or something for the Lifetime Channel."

"Sure, there are plenty of women's problem pictures. But you gotta be a woman with a problem. Like you gotta be a sex psycho murderess, or a poor schleppy broad with a need to suffer. You, you're normal."

"Okay, I'm not saying I'm totally normal, but for argument's sake, I'll concede I am disgustingly ordinary, and I do see your point. So I'm normal, but I'm not boring!...I'm...well..." I wrack my brains for something nice that people have said about me. "I'm witty! Yeah. You remember, Morgan Sidney was famous for her one liners."

Bernie shakes his head. Clearly I don't get it.

"Yeah, but for movies today, they don't want wit, they want a smart ass—with attitude up the Kazoo."

"Oh." Pause. I really don't do attitude. I tried once and looked completely asinine. "Well, how about a sensitive, touching film? I've very sensitive to people's feelings."

"But you're not neurotic. You know, a weepy, wet nosed, tearing up, victim type."

I draw back from that unpleasant picture.

"No, no, I'm not a cry baby. I'm reasonable and forgiving to a fault, and then I go for the jugular. So you see, I can be intense," I assert forcefully, fixing him with my 'intense gaze'. Hey this is my future we're talking about here.

Bernie just shrugs. "But you're not a fanatic. Today intensity is not enough. You have to be ready to kill someone horribly, or drive off a cliff in despair. Or you have to look depraved enough to be a blood sucking vampire. You know what I mean?"

"Yeah, I know, vampire means no blondes, brown hair, or redheads. They want a real brunette with dark eyes. So subtle." I pause thoughtfully. "How about a career woman? I could play a career woman."

"You're not driven. Movie career women all want to be the President, or the world's greatest surgeon, and nothing less will do. They're single minded, hard driving, arrogant, pushy, and they never cry. Ambitious in the extreme. You're too nice. So you see what I mean..."

"Wait a minute," I pipe up. "TV Guide said I was sexy. I'm sexy. Not a bimbo, but sexy."

"But you're not a slut!—and I'm glad about that—but sexy isn't enough, just won't cut it."

"They said I was sexy and that I work great with men. Guys were always dying to do a guest spot on my show, because I made them look good."

Leaning across his desk, Bernie gives me a look of fond exasperation. "Where have you been? Women today want vengeance against men." He pauses. "Look, your show was a hit. Women liked you. Men liked you. You made the studio and the network a lot of money. And they don't care, not even about the money. They're all locked into some modern agenda. Show biz has become some sort of a soapbox for all these Hollywood nuts to stand on and shout their opinions from. They want to make America as screwed up as they are, God forbid. But people have to watch something between the beer and car commercials." He picks up the casting sheets. "Kiddo, I've been through these casting calls a thousand times. There isn't anything. You'd just be wasting your time and money. It's a crazy business."

In desperation, I grab the casting sheet out of his hand and flip through it. "What about this one? The thirty year old intimidating career woman with a cat?"

"Already cast. For 'confident' read 'ball breaker'. They said you weren't strong enough. They cast some Southern broad with a voice like a hyena and a hard on for the entire masculine sex for expecting her to be Scarlet O'Hara. Dear God, save me from those neurotic Southern Belles."

I drop the sheet and dig into my handbag for a cigarette. "Do you mind?"

"You quit. But it's a tough day. Go ahead."

I inhale, trying to take it all in. "So what you're saying is that I'm a good actress, I have talent and experience, and you believe in me, but..."

"You're unemployable. Now listen to me. I've known you since you were a sweet little kid. Take my advice. You're the kind of woman who should get married, settle down, and have babies. You've had a good career, and you'll make a great wife and mother. Marry Justin."

"Justin is dating Melissa Jones," I reply glumly.

"The girl who got your time slot?" Bernie howls in disbelief. "Well, maybe I was wrong; you are a woman with a problem—you're stupid." I give him a grim look. "Aw, no kiddo, I don't mean it. You'll find somebody who—and this is very important—who is NOT IN THIS BUSINESS! You'll settle down and be happy. Find a guy to share your life with."

With a clarity born of total panic, I get an idea. "That's it! How about a movie like that? Two normal people trying to live life together."

"What? A wife, happily married? Where's the story? That wouldn't even make a good documentary."

"Listen, I think I'm on to something here. Maybe something no one ever thought of before."

"I doubt it," Bernie says, leaning back in his chair and getting ready to hear me out. "But go on, tell me your idea."

"I don't know this from firsthand experience, of course, but it seems to me that no marriage is ever perfect. It isn't exactly an uneventful, trouble-free institution. Half of all marriages end in divorce. Something must be going on. What about a movie like that?"

"Two people bickering? Would that be fun to watch?"

"Well..." I continue, now truly inspired by my own brilliance. "Try this. Two *normal*, but interesting, people facing and solving the difficulties of falling in love and staying in love, and getting through life together."

Bernie frowns thoughtfully. "Put that way, it has possibilities. But I don't see scripts like that anymore."

"Anymore!" I exclaim thunderstruck. "You mean there used to be scripts like that?"

"Sure. In the old days, movies like that were called romances." (I stifle a groan. I wouldn't be caught dead in a romance picture. But I listen politely, anyway.) "They were a staple at the box office. My great uncle Bernie, who I'm named for, did bit parts in a lot of romantic comedies. He was a pretty well known character actor. Oh, it was great stuff. I loved it. Two people discovering the fun and adventure of life and falling in love." Bernie's eyes grow misty with a faraway look as he reminisces. Even though I already have objections, I indulge him in his little trip down memory lane. "Gosh, I'd almost forgotten about movies like that. They haven't made films like that in years. These days, you walk out of the theater deaf from the gunfire and explosions, and the violence gives me a headache. When I was young, my sweetie—we're celebrating our forty-second anniversary soon, you know—we used to go to the movies together. We'd walk out of those movies feeling great, like somebody had waved a magic wand over life and suddenly it looked pretty good. But, today, Good God, we never go to the picture show together. I have to sit through tons of crap for business reasons. But everything on the screen today is more depressing than the evening news."

I smile at my pal Bernie, with his Hollywood tan and slightly fleshy face, that's somehow more attractive for being well used. And his big, Mr. Success grin is as winning as ever. I fall a little in love with the guy all over again. What a die-hard romantic! What a heart of gold! What a guy! What a bunch of clichés that all seem to come to life so brilliantly when applied to him.

"Oh. Bernie," I sigh wistfully. "Romance movies aren't like that anymore. Now they're just soft-core porn— bodice rippers—silly female fantasy fluff for sex starved housewives. Doing romance would really be the end of my career. At least, playing a detective was not embarrassing. Detectives are serious, important people. Today, romance is just dumb."

"Well, it didn't used to be. But hey, forget it. Those days are gone. Nobody, and especially nobody in *Hollywood*, cares about staying together. Everybody wants a new partner every fifteen minutes. Marriage doesn't interest Hollywood. Why would it? They stink at marriage." Then, doing his very good Bogart in *Casablanca* imitation, "You want my advice, go back to Peoria."

He humors me awhile longer, as I desperately try to come up with some way to continue my acting career. It's hard to accept that there's nothing, no future for me. I've learned so much during the last five years that I feel like I could do even better things, if I could just get the chance. I suggest Sci Fi, but you've gotta be a pretty bad actor for that. Horror? Just a lot of screaming. Comedy? All gross out stuff. He promises me he'll be on the lookout for something, anything. And I promise to really think seriously about... (gulp)...retiring. He's sympathetic; I'm tearing up.

There's really nothing to say. Bernie's right about show biz. He's always right. Somehow, I can't accept it all at once. A small increasingly distant voice in my head keeps saying 'this can't be happening to me.'

As we stand up and head for the door, Bernie assures me he'll keep his eyes open for parts for me.

"You never know. Maybe something will come along," he says soothingly. "Why don't we go to lunch tomorrow? You pick your favorite restaurant. Oh, and I almost forgot. I got them to give you your wardrobe from the show. It isn't usually done, but friends of mine pulled strings. I know Morgan wore a lot of jeans, but in five years of wardrobe, there ought to be a few good things you can use. Some designer suits, evening gowns, coats, shoes, expensive stuff to fill out your own wardrobe."

I brighten up a little. "Hey that's great. Thanks a lot, Bernie. I'll be the best dressed housewife in Peoria."

"But the catch is, you've got to pick the clothes up today. Right now, in fact. Otherwise, it might all get sent to the warehouse. My friend stashed the clothes in a dressing room on one of the old stages they don't use anymore. She's got boxes there for you. Just pack what you want in the boxes, tape them shut and address them to yourself; and nobody at the studio will ever notice they're gone. They're in the main dressing room near the entrance of stage 24A on Loretta Young Drive. Here's a map. It's a hike, but you'll find it. She'll take care of everything."

I thank Bernie again. And I'm suddenly even more crushed, realizing that they've already cleaned out my dressing room. *Morgan Sidney* is so over. Boo hoo hoo! Bernie gives me a big hug, and then I duck out of the building, before I start to cry for real.

Chapter Two

Shock has a wonderfully numbing effect. I step out into the California sunshine just like this was any other day. I see activity picking up all around. Golf carts buzzing and bumping by me. Across from the little orange tree plaza, the four-story, industrial size entryway, called the elephant doors, to one of the stages is open. I hear the sound of hammering and the buzz of voices of the legion of people whose names will appear on the twenty-minute crawl at the end of whatever movie they're working on—the crawl that only Hollywood people stay to watch in its entirety, anymore.

I light up, *again*, and lean on my car to watch. Peering inside the stage, I see what appears to be a huge science fiction set version of a landscape on another planet. This is, no doubt, another of those mega budget blockbusters, the kind where the special effects are not only the star of the movie, but the only reason to bother to see it. And I'm sure, once they've filmed all they can on this alien planet setting, the next big thrill will be filming it getting blown up or wasted in some spectacular way. The human star of the movie will be some likeable, already famous guy, helped out by a suitably attractive girl and perhaps a kid and a couple of character actors, none of whom, except the star, will in any way detract from the scenery.

I stub out my cigarette and wonder why an intelligent person like myself would stay in this business. Well, I'd better go get those costumes so I've got something to show for the last five years of my life. I set off on foot, leaving the Mustang slumbering under the orange trees, and head deeper into the maze of stages and storage sheds. The stage I'm looking for is on a part of the lot I've never been to before.

The walkways between the gigantic stages are in deep, cool shade, which makes my hike very pleasant. It's quiet, since no one much frequents this area anymore. The only time they ever use one of these old buildings is when there are hundreds of extras who need a place to be gotten into makeup and costume.

As I amble along with the sorry feeling that I'm really going to miss all this, all I can think is 'retire'. I can't get that damn word out of my mind. It's so final. Bernie could have kept submitting me for years and let me find out for myself that I'm not what they're looking for. But he likes me too much not to give me a head's up, so I don't fritter away all my money. And I think he may be right. Truthfully, I can't remember being at a movie recently where I saw some actress playing a part that made me think 'Wow! I wish I could have played that role'. I just seem to be the wrong actress in the wrong place at the wrong time.

Following the map, I stroll by some colorful, oversize boxes of bright flowers, and around a few corners before I find myself on Loretta Young Drive where stage 24A is supposed to be. But Loretta Young Drive is approximately a football field long, with only a back entrance to stage 24A. Consulting the map I see that the main entrance is on Rin Tin Tin Drive, which looks to be a long walk from where I am. It's only a short walk to the back entrance, which is probably locked, but I decide to try it anyway. I'm in luck; it's unlocked.

Making sure the double, soundproof doors are unlocked so I can get out if I need to, I venture into the solid, old stage building. As my eyes adjust to the gloom, I realize it's quite cool inside, in spite of the heat outside, proving they knew a thing or two about clever building tricks to keep cool in the bad old days before air conditioning. There must be a dust-covered, old window somewhere, because the stage is bathed in a drab gray light, which enables me to make out all the dilapidated props, scenery, and worn out film making gear that litter the vast interior. For a long moment, I stand by the door, reluctant to go any further. The semi-dark, the dust, the cobwebs, and the faint odor of mildew that says this place hasn't been opened in years, all seem uninviting, and even sort of scary and dangerous. It's probably wisest to just go back outside and take the long way round. But I don't feel wise today, I feel rebellious.

I've never been on one of these old stages before, never even bothered to take the studio tour. And now I find myself in one of Hollywood's forgotten attics, full of treasures from a glorious past. It's like finding old pictures of your grandmother and discovering she was a showgirl in skimpy costumes with great legs before she met your grandfather. I just can't pass up this incredible opportunity of being let loose in a museum after closing time. A chance like this may never come my way again. As I look around at all this old paraphernalia from another age, I'm reminded that they've been making movies out here for a long, long time—about a century, in fact. And this was one of the first old studios. This place could be as old as 1925. Flappers could have Charlestoned right on this stage. Silent cowboys could have made love to silent heroines right where I'm standing.

I do see a few things that haven't changed: a canvas director's chair, a couple of tall wooden stools, the matchboxes, (about four inch high, wooden boxes with hand holds that can be piled up so actors of different heights will look okay together on camera) forty pound canvas sandbags to keep things in place that the crew refer to as bon bons, and the all too familiar, python size cables, perfect for tripping over. Huge old Klieg lights, with their barrel shaped heads drooping down, stand on their rolling tripods like giant sentinels waiting for their cue to come to life. Oh boy, I'll bet they were hot to work under. Along the wall, there are painted scenery flats. I pass one from a diner set, which looks very convincing with its use of perspective and appropriate shadows to create a three dimensional appearance. A sign in the diner reads "Blue Plate Special .35 Cents". All that's missing is a smart aleck waitress serving lousy coffee, and the hardboiled detectives in dark suits and hats.

I see a door on the far wall and head for it. Before leaving, I glance back one more time. This really is hallowed ground for anyone in show biz. I try to imagine this place full of actors and actresses, (There were actresses in those days—great actresses.) cameramen, directors, crew, and all the people who make the magic of the movies possible. What triumphs! What tragedies! What heartaches and wild, red hot love affairs came and went here, in that bygone era.

But at last, as they used to say in Hollywood, I must bid a fond farewell and be on my way. I push through the far door, and it does indeed lead to the hall with the main entrance down at the end, and there are dressing room doors all along the stage side. My costumes are supposed to be in the dressing room by the entrance, but the first door I pass has a star on it, and I can't resist peeking in. It's probably empty, but who knows? Maybe an old Max

Factor lipstick tube will be lying around, and I'll have a souvenir.

I push the door open and feel around for a light switch and flip it; but there is no flicker of ugly, greenish fluorescent overhead. Instead, the room is instantly bathed in warm, bright, lifelike light, and I can't believe what I'm seeing. It's a fully furnished dressing room. There's a chaise lounge, a vanity table with the classic bare bulbs framing the mirror, and a thick cushioned satin stool to sit on while you do your hair and make-up. But the very best surprise is a rolling rack of evening gowns, dresses, and suits, and a shoe rack of dressy leather shoes.

I'm stunned. This dressing room must still be in use, or used very recently. It must be for the extras on some big production. Boy, these extras really have it good. This is as comfortable as the trailer I had on *Morgan Sidney*.

What better way to procrastinate on my last day than to take a minute and poke around to see what I've been missing. The vanity table has a big kit of very unusual, vintage cosmetics: 'Gardenia' white face powder that I've never seen before; Helena Rubinstein mascara; Westmore pancake in ivory, with a touch of pink; and Max Factor lipsticks in all shades. I can't believe my good luck.

Proceeding to the clothes rack, I pull out one of the evening gowns. It's gorgeous and made of white satin that's as heavy as velvet. It's bias cut, to accentuate a girl's curves, and backless—very sexy. Another gown is a dazzling, spaghetti strapped, mint chiffon number with a cascade of floating ruffles for the skirt. And there's an emerald green velvet, ribbon trimmed, medieval style drop waist gown with a matching hooded cloak. I'm breathless with excitement and envy. Boy, to wear these costumes and do a scene! What fun that would be!

I'd love to know what film these are for, and what lucky extras get to wear these costumes. It even crosses my larcenous brain that I could stick these gowns in one of my *Morgan Sidney* boxes and keep them. They are certainly much better than anything poor, hard working Morgan ever got to wear.

On to the shoes! They're all thirties style, Ginger Rogers pumps and strappy sandals in satin and, ohmygod! real green snakeskin! Oh, I could faint. This is too tempting.

I've just gotta try on at least one of these gowns. In a quick five minutes, I'm in the satin backless gown, wearing the silver crisscross-strapped sandals and ready to rumba. I perch on the satin stool in front the mirror, slick my hair with some sort of brilliantine gel and give myself high arched brows, deep cheekbones, and a dark red mouth, a bit bigger than my real mouth. I pause to admire my handiwork in the perfect light around the mirror. Wow! I look so Hollywood Hurrell, glamour shot ready! Humming a bar of "Let's Face the Music and Dance", I can just see me and Fred fox-trotting around the stage. I stand up and try a few steps. It's thrilling! The heavy satin skirt does divine things when you move. Even I look as graceful as a gazelle. I certainly wish I was working on this film, even as an extra. It would be a dream come true.

I'm mid spin when there's a tap on the stage door, and someone calls 'five minutes!'

Oh, oh, they've caught me. But whoever is supposed to be here, obviously didn't get their call and has missed her cue by a long shot. And anyway, doesn't that door lead to the empty stage I just walked through? Well, these old stages are so confusing, it could lead anywhere.

I can't decide whether to strip quickly and run for it, or what. Suddenly, I have a better idea. Why not *be* an extra on this film? Some of the crew may recognize me, but so what? I'm an actress, I know what I'm doing, and it might be a real hoot.

I crack the door cautiously and look around. It turns out to open into the actor's green room, where performers relax between takes. Opening the door further, I see two male extras lounging around the nicely appointed green room. One is a very good-looking guy in a tropical white, navel uniform and captain's hat. He's tan with a day's growth beard darkening his chin and a natty, sleek moustache. I can't help thinking we'd look great together, dressed as we are.

Lounging with his feet up on the plush sofa, he grins at me.

"Excuse me," I ask with a friendly smile, "are you waiting for someone?"

His grin widens. "I've been waiting for someone like you all my life."

Flattering actor bullshit, but no help. Best to put this overly familiar guy in his place right away. "Get a grip. Somebody knocked at my dressing room door and called five minutes. I was just trying to help."

The other man, who has been shaking ice in a silver cocktail shaker, is also good looking, but in a more sophisticated way. He's very well dressed in a smart, dark suit, white shirt and tie. Over his shoulder, as he fills a couple of martini glasses, he says:

"Ignore him! He thinks no woman can resist his charms." He turns and offers me a martini, and without hesitation I take it. Hey, this has been at least a one martini day. "Have one of these, before you go on. Nothing helps one's mood like a cold, dry martini."

"Are these real?"

I take a sip and answer my own question. They're real, alright.

He offers me a cigarette, and for the first time, I notice the other guy is smoking, too. And he has one of those wonderful, hard to find, vintage, freestanding ashtrays beside him. Boy, I could get used to working on this set.

"Thanks," I reply, taking the ciggie he's lit for me, inhaling deeply and knocking back more of the martini than I should. "So, what are you filming here? I didn't know there was a period picture shooting on the lot. I work over on stage 10. Maybe you recognize me, I was Morgan Sidney."

The sophisticated man gives me a puzzled look.

"The TV show. Morgan Sidney, PI. Surely you've heard of it." Are these guys getting cute with me? Everyone in the industry has at least *heard* of my show.

The big guy gets up, and he's even bigger than I thought. Extras are never that tall. This guy is going to tower over the star of this film, no matter who he is. He's well built, too, a real hunk, if there ever was one.

"Sorry, never heard of it," he comments with a blank look, putting me thoroughly in my place. "Come on, sister, they're waiting for us on the set. Follow me." He says this like it's all a joke. Then giving me the once over with his ravenous eyes, he loops my arm in his. "You sure look swell."

"Thanks," I reply, trying not to be all shook up. But this is the guy who could do it.

A Rogue, A Pirate, and A Dry Martini

I go along with him. I guess one extra is as good as another. If anybody notices, I can explain later. We enter the very busy set. The usual scruffy crew men are dragging cables, hoisting overhead lights, and holding microphone booms on their long poles at the ready. The cinematographer is perched behind the camera on its dolly, (the wheeled carriage that moves it.) The director stands nearby looking thoughtful. He glances at me, smiles, and goes back to staring at the set, so I guess I'm home free.

The set is the interior of a captain's shipboard cabin: very nice with lots of wood paneling, a sofa, a desk, louvered door, and a deck railing outside. Looking around, I wonder where the other extras are, but maybe we're a couple whose shadowy forms pass across the door slats in the background. We walk onto the set, and before I can ask what I'm supposed to do, the clapboard sounds, and the director calls 'Action.' Then the big guy grabs me in a tight embrace and starts to try to kiss me.

"Hey, wait a minute! Don't get funny with me, pal. I don't fall for that stuff." I fight my way out of his arms—reluctantly, I admit. I'm waiting for the director to jump in. Two extras cannot be kissing center stage. No, no, that never happens. But the director says nothing. And the big guy is completely unfazed. He puts his foot up on a stool, casually resting his crossed arms on his knee. Boy, he looks absolutely delicious, all in white with that sexy five o'clock shadow. There isn't a leading man in Hollywood who can touch this guy for looks and sex appeal. And he's an extra. What a crazy world!

"No, Dolly," he chuckles easily. "You never did fall for funny business. That's why I like you so much. Now honey, you know I'm the best Captain in the Archipelago.

Marcy Casterline

I work the Malay Ocean from Hong Kong to Singapore. Never lost a ship. But this is Alan, your boyfriend, talking to you, not Captain Gaskell. It's time for you to jump ship. And I don't care if you *do* have a job in Singapore. It's like this, sister, you and me have had some pretty swell times together, but I'm not sure I can stomach this lousy corner of the world much longer. I know you think we're made for each other. And it's true, honey, you fit in, you're fun, you're cute."

"Cute?" I sneer. "Where have you been, buster? You can't talk down to me. Women are not cute."

He laughs, looking completely irresistible.

"Cute, neat. You can take care of yourself. You have some smarts. I think I'm pretty cute myself."

"I'll bet you do." I try to sound mad, because I should be, but the way he looks at me, and knowing how sexy I look in my satin gown and glamorous makeup is just, frankly, an erotic fantasy come to life, but with a plot I can't figure out. Besides, I'm sure the director will jump in any moment and break up our little tiff, so we can get on with shooting the scene. We're probably waiting for the principals to come on set and do their thing.

"Like I said, you're cute." His steady gaze keeps me absolutely in his power. I can't move or take my eyes off him. "You're my number one girl. But here's the scuttlebutt. A woman from back home is aboard, and she's come around to thinking that losing me was a mistake. She's a real lady; and well, I guess I'm falling for her all over again. So you and me...it's not looking too good. I know you're steamed. Go ahead, let me have it!"

My hopes are dashed. There's another woman. Darn. I look so great, too. But why is he telling me all this? Extras don't have story lines.

"So?" I say defiantly. "Who needs you? I'm better off without you."

"Of course you are. But I know you're crazy about me, and..."

"The only way I'd be crazy about you is if I was crazy!"

He grins that annoyingly confident grin, the one that makes me want to slap him, before I kiss him. Then he comes over to me and holds me by my arms, looking serious and sympathetic at the same time. "Well, honey, you always did seem a little goofy to me."

"Oh yeah? Well, look at yourself. You're no prize, either."

"So why are we having this discussion?" he asks with surprising gentleness. "Why don't you get off my ship? I never made any promises."

Now I'm really pissed. He can't order me around. And for some reason, the camera is still rolling. But I refuse to let this stuck-on-himself guy have the last word.

"No, that's right. And I didn't ask for any, did I?"

He looks abashed, and I feel great.

"No, honey, you didn't. I'm sorry, but..."

"Sorry! You're making a big mistake. You can't just walk out on me."

"Oh yeah?" he suddenly looks cold and hard. "Watch this."

He abruptly lets go of me and exits the cabin. I'm left on the set alone. Hello? Now what?

"You dumb fool!" I yelp. "What am I supposed to do?"

In frustration, guided by years of playing scenes, I opt for a big finish. I grab a small metal ashtray and hurl it at the closed door, making a loud crash, aided by the special effects guy.

"Cut!" The director calls. At last.

Suddenly the stage is engulfed in activity. As I stand a moment, breathing hard and shaking with excitement, they start picking up the furniture and striking the scenery flats. Still in a huff, I march over to Alan, who is waiting for me just off camera. I'm primed and ready to continue the battle.

"You were great," the big sap says with such engaging sincerity that I know he really means it from the heart. Once again, he wraps my arm in his and escorts me back to the green room.

"I was? What's going on here?"

"Same thing as usual, baby, except when we work together, it's always electric. Come on, kid. You've gotta get changed."

"Changed?" I mutter, in complete bewilderment.

In the green room, the suave guy is waiting with a fresh martini, and holding the cute little chiffon number that I saw on the clothes rack a few minutes ago.

"Go on and change. The wardrobe mistress just pressed this for you. Your martini will be waiting for you when you get back."

I dash into my dressing room and throw on the new gown. I'm so eager to see what it's like to play a scene in this mint stripped, floaty chiffon dress, that I don't care about all the questions buzzing in my head.

Back out, and Mr. Sophisticado hands me my martini. After a few sips, I don't really care what's going on here. I'm having more fun acting than I've ever had.

"That martini will calm all the reckless emotion old Captain Heartthrob always inspires. No man is worth it. Least of all, me," my well dressed, new scene partner says with a sardonic grin that I could fall in love with.

We head back to the stage and a new set is all prepped for us. It's a luxurious, upscale, Art Deco living room, complete with a picture window view of the New York skyline. It's spacious and elegant, and I in my chiffon and Mr. Sophisticado in his tux are dressed like we belong here.

"So, what gives here?" I whisper to my drinking buddy, while he pours me another martini in a new prop glass. "Are they using us to block the scene for the principals? Where are the stars?" He smiles quizzically at me. "Oh, wait!" I say, suddenly getting an idea. "Is this some new kind of reality show about making a movie? Something like 'America's next big movie star'?"

He chuckles and downs his martini. "It's a kind of game we play here. We talk, they film it, many skilled craftsmen turn it into a movie, and people pay to see it. Very strange, but fairly lucrative," he answers me, with that sardonic grin again. It's impossible to get this guy to be serious. But after all these martinis, who can be serious?

"Action!" the director calls.

"I know that look," Martini man says archly. "You're dying to ask your little Nicky about the young lady at the bar who threw her arms around my neck in that *fatherly* fashion."

"No, no I don't care. Somehow, I trust you...Nicky." The name and this art deco set ring a distant bell and seem somehow familiar, but I can't place them.

Nick sits down on the smoothly curved sofa, a real vintage Deco masterpiece. "Now don't go all respectable on me, all of a sudden," he says playfully. "I like you better when you're my vivacious, redhead with a wicked temper."

Marcy Casterline

"Oh, I get it, Nick. Don't worry about me. I've got this kind of part down pat. It could be my life story. I'm the victimized good girl, the one who loves you to distraction, (and your money doesn't hurt either). But you just can't be faithful, right?"

With that marvelous smooth smile of his, he takes my chin fondly in his hand. "Ah, I see you've been reading cheap dime novels again, darling. But, all right, we'll play it your way. She and I are having a torrid affair. Every night, I pretend to go to sleep peacefully beside you, but then I sneak out and meet her to make furious and desperate love to her. And beware! When I say I'm working late, I'm not pouring over reports, but cold martinis for Lulu. And what gives me the energy for all that frantic activity? Why nothing else but your good cooking."

"I cook?" I exclaim in surprise and disappointment. "All dressed up like this?"

"You see my point." He raises his glass in a toast to me. I'm really lost about what's going on here. It reminds me of the old improvisation exercises I remember from my acting class days. But in those exercises you were always trying to provoke emotion. Here, wit seems to count for a lot. Well, I can be witty, so I'll go on playing my trump card as best as I can, and maybe I'll win the reality show contest, or at least be amusing.

There's a knock at the door.

"Would you mind getting that, darling," Nick says. "I'm rather tired lately; I can't imagine why."

"Humm," I reply, raising a brow and giving him a knowing look. "Lulu, I suppose." I head for the door. I can't wait to see what happens next. I open it and there's *Bernie*, of all people. But is it Bernie? It looks just like him, but something is different; maybe it's the pancake makeup. He's dressed in a trench coat and hat, looking great. Before I can say anything, he pushes past me and goes directly for Nick.

"Well, Nick," he growls. "You said you'd level with me, tell me everything, if I told you everything."

Bernie's pretty good, but that's no surprise, really. He comes from a theatrical family and besides, Bernie's always played fast and loose, even as an agent.

"Hey," I say slyly, moving to Bernie's side. "Is this one of those buddy pictures you were talking about? He's the sophisticated one, and you're the tough guy?"

Bernie does a double take to Nick and me, and Nick shakes his head sadly.

"You have to excuse her, Three Fingers, she's making fun of us. Two men of the world like us would never waste their time being buddies with another man."

"Three Fingers? Who has a name like that?" I chortle, delighted by the whole game.

"You remember, darling, Three Fingers McGirk. He helped us with the case of the purloined passport."

"Oh, right," I play along. "What case are we on now?"

"Darling, I think Three Fingers needs a drink of water from the kitchen." He indicates the kitchen door with a nod of his head. I start to go, but Three Fingers looks menacingly at me and steps between me and the door.

"You stay right here. I know your tricks, Nick. She'll go in the kitchen and call the cops cause she knows you're in a spot. Why didn't you tell me Lulu was in town?"

Nicky shrugs casually. "Because I haven't figured out yet exactly what Lulu has to do with you."

"Nothing, if she's smart," I say, getting into this. Mystery and detectives have been my bread and butter for five years. But I never had a partner like Nick. Poor me.

"Don't talk about my Lulu like that!" Three Fingers erupts.

Nick smiles in satisfaction. "She's your girl, eh, Three Fingers." Nick pauses and looks solemn. "I'm sorry to be the one to tell you this, but Lulu is dead. I visited the morgue this afternoon to identify her body for the cops."

"Lulu's dead?" I exclaim. I love a murder mystery.

Suddenly Three Fingers pulls out a gun and points it at Nick and me, slowly moving closer to us with a very determined look.

"See, she don't believe Lulu's dead, either. Are you two-timing both of us, Nick?"

Under my breath, I mutter, "So much for the buddy picture idea."

Three Fingers hears me. "Nicky used to be my buddy, but now he's lying to me about Lulu. " He brandishes the gun in Nick's face. "Now tell me where she is."

Nick remains totally cool and calm, never for a moment losing his martini dry, sophisticated delivery. He's totally unflappable. I love working with this guy. He's always one step ahead of me.

"Three Fingers, that gun is looking awfully dangerous. You wouldn't want to shoot me by mistake. You'd never find out where Lulu is."

In a flash, Three Fingers points the gun in my face.

"Maybe I'll shoot her!"

I roll my eyes, strike an elegant pose, and play for time. "Oh, for Pete's sake! Shoot me? Aren't you forgetting that I'm the powerless female? Why *shoot* me, when there are so many amusing things to do to the victimized woman? Tie her up...rip her clothes...menace her." I've got his full attention now. His jaw has dropped. He looks shocked.

Quickly taking advantage of Three Fingers' momentary distraction, Nick does a stage fake roundhouse punch at *my* jaw. I dodge it by instinct, but the sound man supplies a resounding Thwack! that will make it seem like it hit home for the audience. And I've lost my balance and tumble to the floor, adding to the believability. Just as I go down, Three Fingers fires. The bullet grazes Nick's arm, but he is already on top of the man, sending him to the ground and the gun flying across the floor. I grab the gun, get the drop on Three Fingers, and rise gracefully to my feet, carefully straightening my chiffon ruffles.

"I'm sorry about that punch, darling," Nick says, rising to his feet and taking the gun.

"Nick, you have a wicked right hook. Why'd you do it?"

"Yeah, Nicky," Three Fingers sneers. "I didn't figure you for the kind of guy to hit his wife. I'd watch out for him, if I was you."

Lighting a cigarette, Nick explains, "Three Fingers is famous for his hair trigger temper, and you, my darling, were directly in his line of fire. I couldn't take a chance. You were great. Under no other circumstances would I harm a hair on your head."

"Hey, don't worry. I liked being part of the action. And I didn't tear my dress or anything. Nicky, you're hurt. Did that bullet hit your arm?"

"It's nothing. Just grazed me. You are the best partner a man could have. You saved my life by playing dumb about Lulu. He was bound to blame me for not telling him she was in town."

"Yeah, why didn't you tell me, you lousy rat?"

Addressing Three Fingers as politely as if he were a respectable banker instead of a hard boiled criminal, Nick is all sympathy. "Because she was with Louis The Gorilla. And, Three Fingers, I like you too much to let you go off after her and get yourself killed. You'll be nice and safe in a jail cell for a couple of days."

"Is she really dead? Just give it to me straight, Nicky," Three Fingers pleads forlornly.

"I'm afraid so. Sorry, McGirk. Darling, will you hold the gun, while I make some more martinis. I think Three Fingers could use one."

"Don't you want me to make the martinis, while you hold the gun? I mean, I'm the one in the evening gown and high heels, right?"

"Darling, Three Fingers know as well as I do that you're a much better shot then I am. But you must admit, no one can touch me for a dry martini."

Three Fingers sinks into a chair, overcome with emotion.

"My sweetie's dead. Make mine a double, Nick. What was she doing with Louis the Gorilla?"

"Maybe they went to the zoo." I'm getting into this flip fast talk.

"Cut!" the director calls. The stage lights go down. A prop man takes the gun out of my hand. Bernie heads off set. The crew starts moving things. I beat a hasty retreat off set, too.

Nicky and I head for the green room. I try to get some answers from him, so that, at the very least, I can puzzle out the plot.

"So, Nicky—you don't mind if I call you that, do you?"

"People have called me worse things."

"Right, so okay. This is some kind of improvised theatrical thing, right? A reality type show?"

"As real as we can make it."

"But you're in on the plot. You've got a script or an outline or something to go by. Are you allowed to tell me what's going on?"

"I'm sure the studio would be thrilled by your eager interest."

"Great. Okay, so this Lulu person didn't know what a good thing she had in Three Fingers?"

"That's right. But the police think Three Fingers killed her to get back the stocks that he'd stolen for her. The ones she was very imprudently using to run away with."

"I can't believe Three Fingers killed Lulu."

"No, neither can I. But we're going to have a hard time proving he's innocent."

"But, Nick, why do we care if Three Fingers did it or not? I mean, why do people like us—sophisticated, rich, educated—why do we even *know* someone called Three Fingers?"

"Three Fingers may not be a paragon of virtue, but he's not a murderer. He really only has three fingers, lost the other two in an accident in the navy. Got a medal, in fact. Now, he's an excellent pickpocket. He has a pension, but he supplements his income by picking people's pockets, often at the race track, where I met him. An unfortunate hobby, which frequently gets him into trouble."

"And Lulu? I don't suppose she's a brain surgeon, either, huh?"

"You're getting the idea. I believe she used to work at Peck and Peck, selling ladies things."

"So she got him into trouble."

"His temper is his main problem. But his temper is nothing compared to Louis The Gorilla's temper. But we'll get to that later."

Chapter Three

Threading our way through the studio, stepping over cables, around sound recording machines, matchboxes and ladders for the lighting men to stand on, and through the forest of lights, I'm surprised that they're actually using all this old fashioned equipment. They've actually gone to great lengths to recreate the look and feel of an old time black and white film. What an interesting idea for a reality show! But I feel right at home. The gear is old, but the business of making movies is still pretty much the same. And the crew is as friendly and cantankerous as ever.

It's a relief to be back in the green room. Someone has put a giant fan in the room to clear out the air and cool it off. It's one of those fans that are often used to create anything from a soft breeze to a hurricane on screen.

Nick goes right for the bar and gets busy with the cocktail shaker. My old buddy, Captain Alan is reclining on the sofa again, so relaxed, so confident, so provokingly attractive. And boy does he know it.

Well, two can play that game, I think, as I sprawl across the plump arm of a large easy chair, hike my ruffled skirt up to my knees and stretch my legs.

"Is poor Captain Alan too tired to sit up?" I simper.

"Wardrobe won't let me sit up in the pants—too many wrinkles."

"What do our characters do for an encore? Beat each other up?"

He ignores me and stubs out his cigarette.

"What's the matter, big guy? Cat got your tongue?" I ask saucily, a bit full of myself after the success of my last scene.

He hops gracefully to his feet, unusual in such a big man, and is suddenly looming over me. This guy is more potent than cheap cologne. He positively takes my breath away. If this weren't a public place...

"No," he says. His voice is as dark and thrilling as chocolate. "And we don't beat each other up. Not our style. But occasionally, when you get out of line, I take you like this. (He hoists me up by my arms and drops me into the chair, then daintily lifts my skirt and drapes it down over my legs.) "Yes, that's better. And now I'm going to tell you to get one thing straight; nobody pushes me around. You can stop throwing yourself at me, because, remember my lady friend? Well, we just did a scene together. Yeah, and without showing any leg, she got me to propose to her. So we're gonna be married, see?"

"Who cares?" I reply airily. "She sounds like a stuck up prude to me." I pull myself to my feet with haughty unconcern and start for my dressing room.

"On the contrary," Alan shoots back, "she's very attractive. But she has some dignity, unlike you."

"How dare you!" I yelp, spinning around ready to knock his block off.

"You know, you're beautiful when you're angry," he purrs. "But you'd better hurry and change back into your slinky satin. Your old pal, Jamesie is waiting for you on the set."

On set, Jamesie turns out to be Bernie, of course. How cool that Bernie is in on this gig. I always knew he had a secret desire to be an actor, and a silly reality show is just the place to make that wish come true. And we'll be working together. He's always kind of had a crush on me, and I guess I sort of have one on him, too.

On set, everybody's ready. Bernie is waiting for me at a small table in the ship's bar. The place is totally Thirties kitsch; frosted flamingoes on the bar's half moon mirror, rattan bar stools, butterfly chairs, and potted palms with long spiky fronds.

The stage manager comes over to us and kneels beside me. Before I can remind him not to get fresh, he's got my feet and is slipping my shoes into little braces bolted to floor under the table. He does the same to Bernie and instructs us that when they start rocking the set, things will slide across the floor. Even our table will move a bit, and we're supposed to grab the edges and pretend to hold it, although it can't move far. Also, we're to use our feet braces to keep ourselves in place.

Oh Shit! Rock the set? What's going on here? He tells us we'll be fine and moves off stage. He walks over to several other stagehands that are all standing by a big piece of hydraulic equipment with pulleys and levers that I hadn't noticed before amid the jumble of movie making gear. Well this is going to be interesting. Rock the set. A ship. Must be bad weather. Is this another remake of *Titanic*?

"Action!"

Bernie, I mean Jamesie, gazes at me with his fond, familiar grin. "Have a drink with your old pal, Jamesie, my little dove."

"Don't mind if I do." I help myself to a glass of what turns out to be ice tea, not Scotch.

"Down the hatch," Jamesie says, and we chug a lug together.

"Helps mend a broken heart, don't it, Dolly?"

"Broken heart? Who's got a broken heart?"

"Aw, you don't have to pretend with me. It's all over the ship that you're crazy about our spit and polish Captain. Too bad he's fallen so hard for that lady-like broad with miles of class. He didn't used to be so snooty, did he? We all had some fun together, then."

"Say, Jamesie, what's she got that I don't?"

"Nothing. Nothing at all. But she thinks she does."

"Yeah, yeah, I know the type. Thinks she's way too good for the likes of us, Jamesie. Dignity? You have to be human to have dignity, and I'll bet she's a cold fish."

If anyone can understand my bitterness, it's Bernie. He knows what I've been through in this business. And no, I'm not thinking of Melissa Jones. She's no lady. Justin would die laughing before he dated a lady. No, it's the Meryl Streeps and the Keira Knightlys of the business that gall me. Meryl, the ice princess, with her fourteen Academy Award nominations. But what's she done that's so great? Where's her Lady McBeth? Or her Blanche Dubois in *Streetcar*? Forget it. Where's the Shakespeare? The Eugene O'Neill? The Moliere? She's never even done George Bernard Shaw, a bit lightweight, but a classic, nevertheless. Meryl had only to lift her little finger and any studio in Hollywood would have come a running to finance whatever she wanted. So, what makes her such a great actress? It can't be her acting, because she's never challenged herself, never put herself on the spot.

And Keira Knightly is on a pedestal just because she's English. Gimme a break! This is the actress who actually managed to turn Jane Austen's beloved heroine, Elizabeth Bennett, into an obnoxious, witless bitch.

A Rogue, A Pirate, and A Dry Martini

Jamesie shakes his head in sympathy. "Women like her make suckers of a lot of men, but not Jamesie. I know what I like, and you've got plenty of it. If you ever get over your fascination for a man in uniform, you can count on me."

I look at Jamesie in pleasant surprise. So, I've got some sex appeal, huh? I guess I couldn't pull off being a satin clad siren if I didn't. And on this set, sex appeal seems to be a good thing.

"Why Jamesie, I didn't know you cared. But who says I'm stuck on the Captain? He can do whatever he wants. Let him make a fool of himself. I don't care."

"Well," Jamesie replies, brightening up, "come into my parlor, said the spider to the fly. Dolly, I'm gonna be a very rich man real soon. You'll see. And I could buy you a lot of pretty things. No more hard work, baby. I'd take care of you. Give up that guy. He's getting too big for his hat."

"Yeah, sure, Jamesie. Let's have another."

When I try to pour the drinks, I notice the set has begun to rock up and down, and side to side, like a slow motion seesaw. It makes me feel like I really am a little tipsy. Jamesie certainly seems crocked. Bernie is doing a great drunk, and that's hard to pull off. He's digging around in his wallet, pulling his money out and kissing it.

"Dolly, look at this beautiful stuff. And it's gonna have lots of company real soon. Look at this!" He holds up half of a torn one hundred dollar bill. "You know what this is?"

"Jamesie, I hope you take better care of the rest of your money," I giggle.

"This, my little songbird, is Jamesie's secret signal. For the pirates."

"Pirates?"

"Malay pirates. They're terrible people. But they're working for me, because this ship is carrying a safe full of gold. Just about enough to retire to the Taj Mahal. And this torn bill matches theirs and shows 'em I'm the inside man."

"You're gonna steal the money? Oh, you can't do that, Jamesie. You'll get into trouble."

The set is really rocking now, and Jamesie and I are hanging on for dear life. I'm feeling pretty dizzy.

"Aw, don't put it like that. In life, you gotta help yourself. I'm just lucky enough to be the guy who knows the pirates who can get the job done."

"But Jamesie, people might get hurt."

"No, no. Not if they do what we tell 'em. We just want the gold. Now, Dolly, you know everything. You're in on this with me, aren't you, you sweet thing?"

"Wait a minute! I may not be a lady, but I'm not a crook—am I?" I sure wish I'd seen a script.

"No, of course not. This is all my job. But you can't tell Alan."

"Oh, if that's all you're worried about. Why would I?"

We're rocking so much, I can hardly think straight, but Jamesie is too drunk to notice.

"That's my girl," Jamesie is patting my hand with more than just fondness, and the look in his eyes tells me he's got more than friendship on his mind. "I bet you'd like to see Alan brought down a peg or two. If we get the gold, it'll ruin him. He'll never get to captain another ship. That makes you happy, doesn't it? Give me a little kiss to show me how happy you are."

He leans toward me, all puckered up. But I'm so queasy that kissing is the last thing I feel like doing, and certainly not kissing Bernie. Much as I like him, actually

A Rogue, A Pirate, and A Dry Martini

kissing him kind of ruins our harmless little flirtation. So I give him our usual quick peck on the cheek, and he glowers angrily at me.

"You gotta do better than that, or I won't believe I can trust you."

Jamesie lunges to his feet and stumbles toward me. I slip my feet free from their stirrups and careen toward a wall railing. Our rattan chairs tumble to the other side of the bar. Jamesie is beside me, holding me, pawing me, trying to plant a wet one on my lips. But I don't care. I'm holding on for all I'm worth to keep from sliding down the rolling set. Jamesie is so drunk he doesn't know what he's doing, and in our scuffle, he drops the torn bill and I dive for it, with Jamesie falling drunkenly on top of me. I stash the bill quickly in my cleavage, and luckily he's so intent on kissing me, he doesn't notice.

Suddenly, the bar door bursts open, followed by a deluge of water and wind. Alan, in a rain slicker and hat, practically surfs through the door on a cascade of water. Outside the door, off camera, I can see a huge wind machine on full blast and two large fire hoses spraying water.

"Well, here come the Marines," I yelp, as I wrestle my way out of Jamesie's inebriated embrace and struggle to my feet. "Let's get out of here."

Jamesie grabs me by the arm, pulling my sopping wet dress half off. I must look sexy as hell, like a wet tee shirt contest. Alan yanks me out of his grasp.

"Hey, you two! You've got to get to the lounge with the other passengers. You'll be safe there. Come on sister," he commands, hoisting me into his capable arms. "It's only a small typhoon."

"Typhoon!" What am I in for? These reality shows always throw you a curve ball to keep it interesting for the audience.

"I guess you and Jamesie were having so much fun you didn't notice."

"Yeah, well, Captain, you've got worse problems than a typhoon." I glance over my shoulder to make sure Jamesie didn't hear, but he's passed out on top of the bar.

Alan half crawls, half carries me out onto the deck. I'm spitting water. My hair is drenched. Thank God for waterproof mascara. Outside is a narrow boat deck and railing, where we're buffeted by more wind and water. To greet us, the stagehands hurl a bucket of water at us, like a wave spume splashing over the deck. Falling back against the ship, I find myself thrown more intimately against Alan.

"I oughta wring your neck!" he barks angrily at me. "I thought you were drowned, washed overboard; and that would have been better than where I found you."

They hose the deck. We slide toward the railing. Alan almost loses his grip on me. If he had, I'd have been drowned on screen and, even worse, washed into the disgusting catch basin off camera that channels the water off stage.

"Looks like you may get your wish. But you wouldn't be so worried, if you weren't still stuck on me, would yah, big boy?"

"Stuck on you?" he howls in protest, getting doused by those helpful stagehands again. "Naw, forget it. I just hate to see you sink so low."

The bucket brigade lets loose again. It's primitive, but effective. I hang on tight to Alan. I'm sopping wet. Not naked—sexier than naked in my slinky dress now pasted to my body. And the funny thing is I'm enjoying this. It's really sexy to be rescued by a cute guy like Alan. Something about him makes this whole experience a real turn on.

"Say," I pipe up, bubbling with good spirits again. "Is the weather always this good?"

"No, I ordered it special for you."

We arrive at the door to the lounge, and Alan drops me unceremoniously to my feet to open the door.

"Wait, Alan, I've gotta tell you something."

I'm still hanging onto him—just for balance, you understand. He gives me a look half furious, and half I-can't-resist-you.

"Aw, shut up and get inside with the others."

"No, this is important, Jamesie..."

"Jamesie again! Is that all you can think about? Get going!" He shoves me through the door. "Just stay in here and see if you can keep out of trouble."

I stumble through the door and he slams it behind me. I'm standing backstage. A whole crew of stagehands in rubber boots, operating pumps, pushing the water down the drain with industrial size brooms, all give me big hungry smiles. Apparently, wet satin beats full frontal nudity in every way.

The backside of the stage set is unpainted plywood and two by fours. Ah, the magic of show business! One minute you're in a typhoon, being rescued by the man of your dreams, and the next, you're a sopping wet actress shivering on a dirty stage being ogled by a bunch of bored, horney stagehands.

I hear the director call "Cut" on the other side of the set. A stagehand gives me a big towel to wrap up in and helps me over the moat and the water hoses. Back around front, Alan is shaking the water off his slicker and handing it to another stagehand. Then he, too, is wrapped up in a towel. We're both drenched. He looks at me and bursts into friendly laughter, and I start laughing too.

"I'm glad *that's* over! Boy, you guys don't mess around, do you? No more typhoons, I hope," I sigh.

Secretly, I wish I could do a Typhoon every week. It's glamorous, that's what it is. Yeah, I know, I'm sopping wet, but it doesn't matter, because everything is so interesting. I'm on a ship in the China Seas; I support myself as some kind of chanteuse, and I'm good at it. I'm daring. I know some fascinating people, and we've had some swell times together. That's glamour! The magic touch applied to life. I love this stuff. I need to freshen up my red, red lipstick for this show. It must be called 'American Glamour Girl'.

"No more typhoons for you, sister. I spent all of yesterday sliding around a wet deck getting hosed and chasing cargo."

"Better you than me," I laugh. He starts for the green room, and I try to follow. "Hey, hang on a minute. I can't walk in this wet dress. Help me, will ya?"

Alan steadies my arm, as, all under cover of my big towel, I peel my wet dress off. He picks up the sodden dress from the floor for me.

"Lucky thing they've got another gown for you. This one is shot."

I wrap myself in my towel, sarong style, and we continue to the green room.

Nicky is lying on the sofa, shooting rubber darts at the mirror over the bar and looking as cool and detached as ever. He's definitely not the typhoon type.

A Rogue, A Pirate, and A Dry Martini

"Hey, is it always like this around here?" I ask, drying my hair with a hand towel.

"Only on good days." His next shot narrowly misses the gin bottle. "Oh dear! That could have been serious. I've got to work on my aim." He reloads and fires again.

Alan strips off his wet shirt, and I try not to stare and pant. He certainly has a great physique. Not the bulging, gym muscle kind of body, more sleek and powerful. No wonder he could carry me around so effortlessly.

"I guess about now would be the perfect time to shoot our sex scene," I suggest, way too eagerly. "I'm all stripped down and ready to slip under the covers with you."

"Our sex scene!" Alan stops drying his hair and stares at me in consternation—real, not fake. "We don't have a sex scene."

Feeling a little embarrassed, I glance to Nicky, who would be just as much fun in the sack, I suspect. "Oh come on, there's always a sex scene. Do we do our sex scene first?"

Nicky sits straight up and puts his dart gun aside, looking equally astonished.

"We do have a scene in our bedroom, but you don't do it in a...towel."

"Of course I don't," I cry indignantly. Do they think because I work on TV that I've never done a nude scene before? "I'll take the towel off, and it'll be just the body beautiful."

Your usual male co-star can't wait for that moment and then tries all kinds of fresh things under the covers, because quite a few are horny jerks who became actors because it was the only way they could get within five feet of a girl. But these two guys don't look so hard up.

They might even be fun to jump in bed with, metaphorically, of course.

"I'm shocked," Nicky says, looking like he means it. "In our bedroom scene, you will be wearing a very lovely negligee. That's what women usually wear, isn't it?"

"Oh, I see." I don't, really. "So, do we do some groping, a little upper body nudity?"

"Well, it's a lovely idea," Nicky responds, with a gently amused smile, "especially for cold winter nights beside the fire. Might just catch on."

Alan has put on a black turtleneck. It's tight and shows off his build to perfection. Looking deliciously irresistible, he frowns at me and says:

"I don't know where you used to work, but we don't do anything like that here. This is a classy studio."

"You don't? After all that hot passion in our last scene, we've been working up to it, haven't we? It's about time we fell in bed and shed our inhibitions, isn't it?" I'm incredulous and very disappointed. For once, a sex scene would be really fun, and these guys act like they've never heard of such a thing.

Laughing heartily, Alan puts his arms loosely around my waist. "Honey, the only bed I want to fall into with you is at home, with soft music, champagne and total privacy."

He's teasing me, of course. I shake out of his grip, and he shrugs and sits down.

"Aw, come on. Every movie's gotta have a nude scene. The public demands it," I sputter in frustration.

"Not my public. I take my shirt off, period. Any more than that and they'd think I was showing off," Alan replies.

"Oh, right," I reply sarcastically. "Well, what about a little hot affection that leads to sex?" I can't figure out what's the matter with these guys. Most actors positively brag about their sex scenes.

Alan smiles slyly. "For me, kissing seems to do the trick.

"Kissing," I scoff.

Nicky comes over to me, because I must be looking a little lost here.

"Yes, kissing. Okay, let me show you." Nicky takes my hand and we're face to face. "Here's how it's done. If I hold you like so, (His hands gently caress my cheeks and draw me toward his lips.) and..."

"I know exactly what comes next. I've done this a few times, myself, too, you know. We look deeply into each other's eyes and..." Then, I go for the total throes-of-sexual-heat kiss so popular in movie kisses these days, giving him the full open mouth, I'm-so-hungry-for-you, let's-have-an-orgasm-now deep tongue kiss. But I've barely begun when he jerks his face away.

"Hold on a second. You have a few things to learn about the art of the kiss. Now backup, and let's start again."

"Okay." I exhale vigorously, trying to relax so I can start again and wondering what I did wrong. "Deeply into your eyes..."

"And I look deeply into yours. I'm thinking how magnificent you are. What a noble creature! What a woman! You're fun and funny. You're one of the gang—honest about yourself and others; you're fair minded and intelligent. You understand so much. You're game for anything in life. The beauty of who you are overwhelms me. I find that mere words of praise are not enough. No words could express what I feel. I embrace you, surround and protect you with my arms. My lips long to tell you how much I love you. Gently, with deep emotion, I engage your lips. I close my eyes to experience the moment fully. And you close yours, too."

We're kissing. Just lips meeting gently in tantalizing desire. It's electric! My whole body goes weak in his arms. The kiss lasts forever, all timeless longing, sublime passion, and overflowing with feverish anticipation of something wonderful to follow.

"I think she gets the idea," Alan interrupts sarcastically, and dare I say it—jealously. Well, he should be jealous. What a kiss! I've sweated myself through forty positions of the Kama Sutra and never felt like this.

Nicky releases me. I manage not to collapse.

"Now you can see that a sex scene is totally unnecessary. It would be a voyeuristic elaboration that could not say more than that kiss. Lesser men may have to take their shirts off, now and then," he says, throwing a condescending smile to his rival.

Alan gives him a dirty look.

"I don't think I've ever been kissed like that before," I murmur, sounding like someone who's just woken up from a trance.

"No," Nicky agrees. "That was clear when you tried to massage my face with your mouth."

"I...I..." I'm too breathless to speak.

"Don't try to talk, you've just been kissed right for the first time. Imagine what other earthly delights are in store for you."

The wardrobe mistress appears at the door to my dressing room, beckoning me to come in and get ready for my next scene.

As I trot off, I call back to Nicky, "boy, I hope I get to do a lot of kissing in these pictures."

Chapter Four

By the time I get to the dressing room, the wardrobe mistress is gone, which is a disappointment. I really wanted to ask her some questions about these shows I'm doing. But she's left me my next costume, and it's a surprise. It can't be for either of the two stories I've been doing, because it's the green velvet medieval gown with a jeweled, gold hip belt. And there's a chiffon snood with a jeweled crown for my head. My loose, towel fluffed, dry hair will look perfect under it. I slip on the dress. What a fantasy come true to get to play a medieval princess.

As I sit down to admire myself in the mirror, I see a note from make-up. 'They're shooting this is color, so use the make-up for color film I've put out for you'. I fix my face with the richer, softer hued color palette and admire myself in the mirror. What a pity I didn't get to talk to the wardrobe or make up people. I wanted to ask them how I can make sure to get in on more of these projects.

At last I'm ready, and I throw the dark green velvet, floor length cape over my shoulders, fasten the jewel neck clasp, and open the door.

The green room is empty. I guess my compatriots are off shooting other scenes, or in their dressing rooms. The stage manager appears and leads me out a side door, off the stage, and out onto the back lot. It's a grassy, tree lined hillside, dressed up with bushes and flowers and flooded with sunshine.

Bernie, in a medieval tunic and boots, and wearing a sword, is seated on the grass with a bottle of wine and a loaf of bread, picnic style. The cameraman and director are in place. The sound booms are overhead. The director gives the cue; they slate and:

"Action!"

Bernie looks up as I amble grandly toward him, my train flowing behind me.

"Well, my lady, in a few hours you'll be in the court of Prince John, your protector in King Richard's absence."

Ah hah! A costume drama. He called me 'My lady'. I really am a Princess. Okay, I confess, I have always wanted to be a princess. Doesn't every little girl? What a job! I actually knew a real live princess once. She stayed with me for a week while Bernie tried to find her a suitable place to live during her LA acting gig. She was a wonderful houseguest, totally fun. The idea of doing something useful with her day never crossed her mind. It was so freeing. Evenings she got me into all sorts of exclusive places that even movie stars can't crash, places where the super rich and the titled socialize strictly with each other. Days were spent either doing pastel sketches of the scenery and views from my front deck, or shopping in marvelous trendy, small and very exclusive boutiques for some delightful or unusual trinket to adorn ourselves with that evening. She completely exceeded my childhood fantasy of the princess game. So now, me, a princess. I stand up a little straighter and walk with regal bearing, befitting my new station in life, then sink gracefully down beside Bernie.

"Oh, how nice. Is he a good Prince?"

"My lady, he is a Norman. I gather the handsome Sir Guy of Gismond will also be waiting for you. I fancy Prince John has plans for you two."

"I see. Well, whatever his plans are, I will choose my own husband," I announce impressively. Hey, I'm a

Princess, aren't I? The job description is royalty gets whatever it wants, right?

"Yes, of course, your ladyship," Bernie replies obsequiously. "But, you will keep an open heart to the advice of your Protector, Prince John."

"I suppose."

"My very good, Maid Marion. You have always obeyed your fealty duties. Now, we must be off. We don't want to dally too long in these woods. Robin Hood and his gang of cutthroats roam and pillage here. But we're safe with our large escort and the Prince's guard."

Robin Hood. Maid Marion. I know this story—sort of. Maid Marion is pure and noble, but probably not in on any of the action. Oh well, I won't get my dress messed up.

"Really?" I look around, but see no one. "Where's the escort?"

"Where indeed! All round us, my lady. Yo Ho! Men! Show yourselves!"

It's all silence on the set, and I wonder if someone has missed their cue.

"Men!" Bernie rises and glances around in concern. "I command you, answer me!" More silence. "Maid Marion, I like this not."

"My friend," I reply, unperturbed; princesses are never flustered. "I think we are completely alone in this forest."

From the treetops above, we hear laughter and:

"No one is ever completely alone in Sherwood Forest."

Bernie draws his sword. "Who said that? Did you hear that?"

"Yes, I believe it came from that tree."

An extraordinarily good-looking man in a green doublet, leather jerkin, and tights swings toward us on a vine. As he leaps down, sword drawn, my heart stops. He is absolutely gorgeous. And how many men could wear such a ridiculous outfit and still look fully masculine and totally sexy? This guy is one in a million. Good old Robin Hood! This must be my lucky day.

"Good day, Sheriff," he says, bursting with good humor, arms akimbo and smiling broadly. "I thought you might enjoy a little practice with your sword. You're always threatening to have me hung, but perhaps you'd prefer to run me through personally. Very well, let's match steel. And to make it more interesting, how about a wager? I take all the gold in your caravan if I win. And if you win, you get to put my head on a pike. Fair enough?"

Instead of replying, Sheriff Bernie lunges at Robin with more grace and skill than I would have thought a hefty guy like Bernie was capable of. They thrust and parry in obviously well rehearsed moves. Robin puts on a great show, very athletic. This explains why he looks so good in tights.

"You brigand! I'll cut your heart out!" Sheriff Bernie hisses, and comes very close to doing just that, but though Robin stumbles, alarming me in spite of myself, he recovers handily.

"That's an operation that would be difficult to perform on you, because you have no heart. But I'll settle for your spleen."

Robin laughs and dances lightly around the Sheriff, at last deftly unswording him.

"Nothing I enjoy more than taking swords from rude Normans! You're a guest in this forest, and I'll thank you not to attack your host again."

A Rogue, A Pirate, and A Dry Martini

"Your guest?" the sheriff snarls. "Never, you Saxon dog! Where are my men?"

"They're my guests, too, at the feast. Won't you join us? And you, too, fair damsel."

He bows with a flourish. I can't help thinking how much I like being bowed to, especially by a handsome man in a doublet. It's quite an attractive outfit for a man with great legs.

Very noblesse oblige, I reply, "Do I have a choice?"

"Why of course you do. You can stay here. But I'm too much a gentleman to let a lady remain alone in the woods. There are wild animals here—mostly the two-legged kind. I'll have to stay by your side to protect you. Actually, the chance to pass a few hours in this green forest in your lovely presence is most appealing." He gives me a meaningful glance, brimming with delightfully wicked intentions.

"You insolent cur!" Half the fun of being a princess is playing hard to get.

"I'm afraid my reputation precedes me. But I take that as a no, you'd prefer to feast with the merry yeomen of Sherwood. Let us be off!"

"You'll pay for this, Robin!" The Sheriff shakes a gloved fist in Robin's direction.

"Alas, I'm afraid the privilege is all yours. We've relieved your caravan of an enormous quantity of gold, good food, and ale. But we Saxons are polite. We'll be more than happy to share it with you."

The Sheriff is livid as he shouts, "that gold is intended for the ransom of King Richard."

"Yes," Robin replies, deadly serious. "It certainly is, and now it will get to the King."

"Are you implying I'm a thief?"

"No. I'm a thief. You're something far worse, a hypocrite. Well, we've organized a little revolt here in Sherwood against your kind. We're going to give some of that gold back to the people who earned it. Now, fair maiden, let us be off. I hear the happy voices of my companions making merry."

Marching in front of us at Robin's sword point, the Sheriff growls darkly, "you'll hang for this Robin."

"Hanging would be a small price to pay for the company of such a charming lady," he replies, glancing at me, his eyes brimming with admiration.

Such over-the-top flattery! But my warmly glowing cheeks tell me this man with his devilish grin certainly has a way with a girl's heart, even when it's all make believe.

"Am I your prisoner, too?" Wow, what a delicious idea to be a prisoner of Robin. Maybe I am in on some of the action, the good stuff. All right, so I'm just as horney as those housewifely romance fans. Maybe I'd like to have my bodice ripped by this Robin. Pant! Pant!

"No, I think rather I am prisoner of your lovely eyes."

"That's the silliest thing I've ever heard, you...you..." Now, I'm breaking the first rule of being a princess and getting flustered, with my heart pounding like mad.

"Impudent rascal? Insolent rogue?" he suggests, laughing uproariously at my flushing face and confusion.

Then he offers his upraised arm for me to rest my hand on as we pass, a grand procession of two, through a thick, bushy undergrowth, followed by the camera and cameraman who are being pushed on a dolly along a track beside us. We enter another set piece where there are long trestle tables. The extras are cued to begin eating and engaging in noisy revelry. Another camera picks up the action on this set, while they reload the first one.

Two merry men lead the Sheriff away, and Robin and I sit side by side at a table. There is a joint of lamb on each of our pewter plates. Must be the real thing, because Robin is gnawing on his.

"Have some food, my lady. You must be hungry from your journey."

"No thank you." I am hungry. Haven't eaten for hours. But leg of lamb, *literally*? No fork. No knife. I'd look like a cave woman. I draw myself up regally, hoping the director will call 'cut' so I can get something more ladylike and more appealing to eat. No such luck. There's no dialogue, either. What are they waiting for?

Robin is eating hungrily, smiling at me, drinking wine from a goblet, and wiping his mouth with the back of his hand. I look at the lamb joint. It doesn't look *so* awful. If I just grip the bones in my fingers, I can do it without looking too uncouth. I lean down for a bite, hoping the camera is panning elsewhere. After a few bites, Robin catches me.

"There, you see, you're not such a conceited Norman. You can enjoy a meal with a Saxon."

Feeling embarrassed and completely absurd in this overwrought costume epic, I throw the leg down. "Please stop! I'm sick of all this masculine bluster."

"Masculine bluster, you call it," he cries in outrage. "Where would the world be without masculine bluster?"

"There's nothing noble or heroic about you and your merry band of lawless ruffians."

Robin leaps up onto the table, scattering plates of food.

Marcy Casterline

"Did you hear that, Saxons?" he hollers to the now attentive crowd of extras in Saxon peasant garb. "The lady says we're not noble, not heroic," he hoists his goblet. "Here's to Richard the Lionheart! Our rightful King. We're going to see that this gold is used to ransom him and bring him back to England! (Deafening cheers erupt.) For England! (More cheers!)"

Robin sits down by me, with my sardonic frown still stuck on my face.

"Oh, Puh leeze!" I whisper.

"My lady," he answers, with his hand gently on top of mine, "would you do less for your country than the lowly peasants? Are you too proud to cheer for your country?"

Put like that, well, I'm a little ashamed. I glance around at the peasants slash extras, who are, if possible, an even more desperate group of performers than actors. I guess I do owe them something. We all need the paycheck.

"Oh, well, perhaps I was wrong, Robin."

"You can cheer for the King when he returns from the Austrian prison," he offers graciously.

I sigh again, letting my gaze rest on Robin's handsome, confident, smiling face. He's really too good to be true. But I can't help falling for this—what did he call himself? Impudent rascal. However, as I recall, Maid Marion is *supposed* to fall for Robin, and I am beginning to understand why; he really is kind of noble. And, dammit! That's very sexy.

Before I can do more than smile demurely, the director calls "Cut, that's a wrap for this scene."

Everybody is once again in motion. I lose Robin in the crowd of Saxon extras and reluctantly return to the green room. It's still empty.

A Rogue, A Pirate, and A Dry Martini

All of a sudden, I'm scared this is over—that we're through for the day, and this may be my only day. Maybe you only get to shoot a few select scenes for this reality show or improvisation contest. Shit! This was all too good to be true. But all good things must end. There's nothing to do but go into my dressing room where it all started. I really hate to leave and be out of a job and going into retirement, again. I'm not ready for that. But, when I open the door, the wardrobe mistress is waiting for me. I could kiss her, I'm so happy.

"You've got a couple of quick changes," she says, all business. She's short and slight with a big raspy voice, belied by a winning grin and mischievous eyes. Her hands are seamstress' hands, thin and sinewy. I notice how deft they are as she helps me out of my medieval contraptions.

"Say, what goes on around here?" I ask, taking advantage of our brief time together. "I've never worked like this before. What are we shooting?"

"We shoot whatever they tell us. So don't blame me. I don't write the scripts."

"No, I mean..."

"I know what you mean, but I gave up asking questions years ago. Some of this stuff seems crazy to me, too. But when they put it all together, it pays the bills."

She helps me into a very revealing flowered silk kimono.

"Now they want your hair kind of tousled and loose. And here's the torn hundred-dollar bill for your pocket. Okay, you're ready. See you in a minute."

She pushes me out the door, and I'm no wiser about what I'm doing than when I went in. But at least I'm still doing it.

Marcy Casterline

Back on stage it's the Captain's cabin set. This time they've added an open door that leads to the captains bunk room. It's night and dark. Alan is sitting on the bunk with a bottle, drinking hard. His hair is all wet like he's just come out of the typhoon. He's wearing a black turtleneck and looks very appealing. What a hottie! So far, three great looking leading men, and all of them seem to have a brain. I *must* be dreaming.

"Action!"

I sidle up to him in the geisha girl kimono.

"Hey, you look exhausted. Wasn't that typhoon awful? I thought the ship was going to sink."

"Darn near did. It was terrible." He pours himself a belt and downs it. He looks tired, done for it. "A couple of passengers in steerage were washed overboard, and there wasn't a thing I or anyone else could do to help them. We were listing so far to starboard I thought we were all goners. I don't mind telling you I was pretty scared."

He pours himself another drink and gulps it down. I gather by the looks of him, this is far from his first drink of the evening. Then I remember the torn bill in my pocket. Pirates. He's still in danger, but given his condition, I'd better be careful how I break this news to him. I sit beside him, friendly and confidential.

"Alan, I've got to tell you something. It's important."

"Get away from me. You've always got one more thing to say. Can't you get it through your head that I'm finished with you? And that's not all. I'm finished with this rotten ship, and rotten life in the rotten China Seas. I'm going to marry Alice and head back to England. She's got enough dough to set us up while I look for something better."

"Yeah, well maybe. But you gotta listen to me." I stare oh-so earnestly into his eyes, and hold his hand in an effort to put the bottle out of the way for a moment.

He pulls the bottle back. "Shut up! Don't try your cheap tricks on me."

Cheap tricks. Right—light bulb overhead. That's my cue. That's why I'm half naked in this sexy kimono. This is my chance to win him back from 'pure as the driven slush' Alice, while I save his life.

"Alan honey," I try to put my arms around his neck, but he flings them away. This isn't going as planned. I'm the sexy girl, everything points that way, my clothes, my drinking with Jamesie, who did say I had plenty of what he liked.

"Get away from me. You're always ready to comfort any sailor, as long as he's too drunk and tired to care. But you won't get me. Not this time!"

"You can't talk to me like that!" Ready to comfort any sailor? What an insult! I'm sexy, but I'm not a hooker. I'm a singer, a chanteuse—a little free and easy, maybe, but I'm my own woman, and I go with a guy because I like him.

"Take your cheap perfume and get outta here." He jumps unsteadily to his feet, but given his size and power, easily manhandles me out of his bunkroom, slamming and locking the louvered door behind me.

"Wait! Wait!" I cry, belatedly pulling the torn hundred-dollar bill out of my pocket. "Listen to me! Look at this! You're in trouble. Alan, open this door. I need to talk to you. You've gotta listen to me, please. Alan!"

"Go away!"

I keep trying to get a response, but he's silent, probably sleeping it off. Did I misread the scene? Maybe the bad girl really is a cheap tart. I don't usually get cast like that. I stuff the bill back in my pocket and turn to go. And Jamesie is right behind me, breathing down my neck.

"What are you up to, Dolly?" He isn't happy. No indeed. He has his hands around my neck, strangling me. He's very serious about this pirate stuff. "You double-crossed me didn't you?"

"No, no..." I gasp, trying to breathe, exaggerating it for dramatic effect, of course. "I was just looking for something." It's a lame excuse, but it seems to work. His grip loosens, and I can breathe again.

"You were? Why of course you were. You know where Alan hides the key to the ship's arsenal, don't you?"

I nod yes, rubbing my sore neck.

"I'm sorry old Jamesie doubted you. You're a smart girl, Dolly. Let's get the key and get out of here."

"Cut!"

I scoot back to my dressing room. My wardrobe lady is ready for me. I shuck the kimono, and it's back to the green chiffon. My detective story continues.

On set, in the elegant Art Deco apartment, Nicky is waiting for me. I no more than take my place beside him, when Three Fingers appears at the door. Bernie has had a quick change, too.

"I didn't expect to see you, for awhile," Nicky says nonchalantly.

"They let me out on bail, so I came here to apologize. I should have known you weren't double dealing me, Nick."

Three joins us on the sofa, between Nick and me. Nick offers him a drink, and when he accepts, goes to the living room bar to fix it.

"Hope I didn't scare you, Mrs. Charles," he says belting down his drink in one gulp.

"Don't give it another thought."

"Nick, are you sure my Lulu's dead? I gotta know."

"I'm sorry, Three Fingers, she is. I'm working with the police to find out who did it. They think it might be Osberg, her rich boyfriend, a scientist inventor type. Seems she'd been helping herself to more of his assets than he was ready to part with."

"Yeah, I know. I helped her steal them. I'll bet the police suspect me. Lulu and I were supposed to leave town together with the loot."

"She made her exit early," Nicky sighs, handing me a drink. "Darling, I'm going to run a little errand for Three Fingers. I'm going to see what I can find out about Louis the Gorilla. Can you hold the fort down till I get back?"

"Wait!" I leap to my feet, floating on a cloud of lime chiffon, and head to the bar for a little private tête á tête. "Before you go, Nicky," I say loudly for Three Finger's benefit. "Why don't you mix our guest another drink?" Then, as he shakes up the martinis, I add, sotto voce. "I want to go with you and get in on the fun stuff, help you track the bad guys and find Louis the Gorilla. You can't leave me behind just because I'm the girl."

Nick leans closer to me, and with a wink and a conspiratorial smile, he says, "I'm leaving you behind just because you *are* the girl. Give McGirk his fresh drink and provide him with a shoulder to cry on. I know you can do it. See you later, dear."

Great. Me and McGirk. The girl serving drinks to a sobbing pickpocket. The emotional scene. Why do girls always get stuck with this sob stuff, instead of important detective work?

Marcy Casterline

"Thanks, Missus Charles. I'm awful upset about Lulu. She was the love of my life. I'm sorry I scared you with the gun."

"Yeah, sure. I understand." Forget Dear Abbey. Even Dr. Phil couldn't help this guy.

"Louis is a real bad guy. I don't know why Lulu got mixed up with him. Poor Lulu, she wasn't a thief; she was only trying to get what was fair. That rich boyfriend thought he could have everything his way. (He reaches into his pocket and pulls out a thick chain link bracelet.) She gave this to me a week ago. Told me to put it somewhere safe. Said it was Osberg's, something he always wore. Poor Lulu."

He starts sobbing his heart out. The phone rings. It's Nicky.

"I'm down in the lobby. Has he spilled the beans to you, yet? I've a got a hunch he knows something he isn't telling. And he's a sucker for a beautiful, understanding woman, accompanied by good scotch. Come to think of it, what man isn't?"

"Yes, dear, we're doing fine here," I say to cover, but inside I feel a glow of pride. I've done it. I got the evidence without having a knock down, drag out match with Louis the Gorilla. I've got my black belt in feminine smarts. So there! Hollywood, Rambo, and the Terminator!

"Good work, dear. I'll give you a few more minutes. Don't want you alone with him any longer than necessary. You're a first class sleuth, darling."

I sit back down by McGirk and pat his hand. He turns his face to me, his brown eyes sad and damp. I know I've got him right where I want him.

"You're so kind, Missus Charles," he says, starring hopelessly at the bracelet in his giant paw. "You know, since my Lulu is really gone, I won't keep this bracelet anymore. It just makes me sad. You keep it, okay?"

"Sure. I'll take good care of it. Don't worry."

"I've gotta go. Tell Nicky I'll be around. I've got some business to take care of."

"All right, but watch out for Louis The Gorilla. He sounds pretty awful."

By the time Nick returns, McGirk is gone.

"He left, Nicky. I did my best to hold him."

"Don't worry. The police are tailing him; and I think I spotted a cop waiting in the lobby ready to tail us, too. What did you get out of him?"

"Take a look at this." I show him the bracelet. "Lulu gave it to him for safe-keeping a week ago. You know, I feel sorry for that man. He's loyal to a fault."

"Yes, and I'm glad it's not our fault, anymore. But what is this?"

"He said it was a gift to Lulu from Osberg. You know, the rich boyfriend. She said it was something Osberg always wore. What does it mean, Nicky?"

"It means we've got to take a little trip. Darling, I'm glad you love me and I love you."

He gives me the look. Oh Boy. Another kiss. A quickie. Just a light tease of lips brushing together. But, Oh! Forget sex, I want more kissing!

"Poor Three Fingers, poor Lulu," I sigh, wondering at the power of love.

"Cut!"

Playfully, arm in arm, we walk back toward the green room.

"Darling," I begin, trying to stay in character. "This is a kind of take off on *The Thin Man* isn't it? Nick and Nora Charles."

"You're getting the idea," Nicky smiles wryly, with a twinkle in his eye.

"It's an interesting idea, but sort of strange. This old fashioned way of working—lots of sets, lots of shooting, old time equipment—something about this seems strange to me."

He shrugs "Seems strange to me, too, sometimes. But who can say? Life is a mystery and people love mysteries. That's why these movies do so well."

Before I know it, with the expert help of my wardrobe lady, I'm back in medieval attire and sitting in a very uncomfortable wooden chair by a huge fireplace, in a room in a castle, with towering stone walls hung with tapestries. Maid Marion at home, I guess.

On Action, Robin leaps through my arched stone window, causing me to jump to my feet in surprise. He takes me in his arms. Wow, if it's time for a kiss, I'm so ready. And from this guy, it should be a showstopper.

"Lady Marion, you believe in our cause now," he says, gazing into my eyes with passionate intensity. "Your handmaiden told Little John you were on our side. I always knew you were a loyal Englishwoman at heart."

"At heart, yes, of course, Robin." Funny he should mention heart. Mine's pounding with anticipation.

"Forgive me for coming and endangering you, but I'm only a weak man. I need the love and inspiration of a beautiful woman."

Boy, they didn't mess around with trivialities in the Middle Ages in old romance movies. None of that 'So, what's up' stuff. It's all love, inspiration and chivalry. This may be my favorite improv of all.

His face is so close to mine, I can almost feel his lips itching to caress mine.

"Just tell me you care, and all the danger will seem as nothing."

"Just tell you I care?"

"Shhh." He hisses and flattens us against the wall, so we aren't visible from the door to my room.

"What! Did you hear someone?" I whisper in alarm. "If they find you here, they'll hang you, Robin. You'd better get away quickly."

He laughs and pulls me close against him.

"You see, you *do* care."

Then he kisses me, and kisses me. Maid Marion is one lucky wench, just a lusty Englishwoman at heart. Boy, these extra guys can really kiss. It's totally sexy, even sexier than foreplay. Thrilling, knee weakening, dizzy with desire. Swoon time.

"I must go now," he draws back reluctantly.

I'm weak in his arms. "Already?" I sigh.

"There are many things to be done in Sherwood." He leaps onto the windowsill. I move toward the window, leaning to him for another kiss. He gazes longingly at me. "I can do anything, now that I know you care. King Richard is as good as freed."

The kiss that saved a Kingdom, and me too. Believe it.

"Oh Robin, be careful!"

"Farewell my sweet maid. I'll dream each night of the day we may be together."

He disappears out the window, and I collapse against the wall, hands clasped to my heaving breast, and it doesn't feel forced or phony. I'm getting good at this. I sigh to myself, 'me, too, Robin, me too'.

There's a loud rap at the door.

"Yes? Who knocks at Lady Marion's door?"

"Prince John, your guardian. Let me in please," he demands impatiently, leading me to suspect he's up to no good.

Gathering my wits, I open the door. There's another actor standing there dressed like a prince, in flowing robes and crown. He's good looking and could almost be a leading man, except for the too shrewd look in his eyes. His expression now is dark and menacing.

"Maid Marion," he says, striding into my room. "I've come to ask your cooperation in a little matter that may eliminate a plague in my kingdom."

"My help, Prince John?"

"Yes. We have been trying unsuccessfully to catch Robin Hood for some time. The Sheriff said that the outlaw took quite a fancy to you, when you were being held in Sherwood Forest. Is it true?"

"I wouldn't know, your highness."

"Well, I would. We're setting a trap for him with you as bait. We'll hold an archery contest, and the winner will receive a golden arrow and a kiss from Lady Marion. I don't see how he can resist."

Poor Robin! He's in danger, and I must warn him.

"Cut."

Chapter Five

The wardrobe mistress is waiting for me. She's steaming the last few wrinkles out of a beautifully tailored tweed suit.

"Is that for me?" I ask, shedding my princess gear.

"Yeah, and I hope you really are size ten like it says on your measurements sheet."

"Of course I am."

"Yeah, yeah, they all say that. Well, here goes nothing. Try it on."

I put the jacket on. "See, perfect fit." They must have been expecting me if they have my measurements. Maybe Bernie set this all up as a going away present.

"Well, I'll be. Okay, here are your stockings and garters."

"Garters?"

"Silk stockings don't stay up without 'em. And here are your shoes."

She hands me a pair of open-toed pumps, and I can't believe it. These are the pumps I saw before, and they are real snakeskin. Incredible, you can tell just by the look and feel. "Wow! Silk stockings, real snakeskin, you really went all out for the totally authentic thirties look."

"Yeah. We don't pinch pennies on wardrobe around here. Nothing but the best."

I re-enter the green room, where Nicky is waiting for me. He looks fabulous, too, in a casual tweed shooting jacket and slacks.

"You look wonderful darling. Perfect for a day at the track. I hope you're not tired. We have our big finish coming up soon."

"Tired? Are you kidding? I've never had so much fun. Every scene, I get to do something new and different; and I get to dress great. And the kissing! You are so right about *that*. I love the kissing. I never really liked all those sex scenes, anyway. I mean where are they going, really? Who cares what happens under the sheets, right?"

So this is the detective story big finish. I guess I've got several big finishes coming up. I can't wait! This is such a fun way to work. I feel I'm really improving as an actress for a change.

We exit the building to that back lot again. The trees are still there, but now it's a racetrack, or enough of a racetrack to fool the camera. There's a railing, track, and pennants flapping in the breeze. And there appear to be horse barns in the distance, which are only scenery flats, but they look very real from here.

Nicky leans against the railing and gazes intently through a large pair of binoculars the prop man gave him before the scene started. Off to one side, the director lines up the shot, and the cameraman gets into place.

"Ready...And...Action!"

"I think we lost our police tail."

"Good. So Nicky, you haven't told me why we're at the racetrack today."

"I love to watch the horses. Maybe they'll run into some black ink for me."

"I see. Gambling's your vice. I suppose you're in hock to the Mafia or something. You're the good detective gone bad. Is that your story?"

"Vice? Gambling's not my vice. My vice is women. Actually just one woman, who has a knack for getting me into trouble."

"Now, how did I do that?"

"You remember that bracelet Three Fingers McGirk gave you?"

"Sure, the one Lulu gave him for safekeeping."

"Yes. I talked to Osberg's daughter. She said it was a sentimental bracelet that her father never took off. It was his good luck charm."

"So? Maybe he gave it to Lulu as a present."

"It was worthless. Made of some cheap alloy he'd invented."

"Lulu doesn't sound like the kind of woman who'd be so attached to a cheap trinket."

"Lulu definitely wasn't the sentimental type."

"I don't get it. So why are we at the race track?"

"Take a look," he hands me the binoculars. "Over by the barn." He points the binoculars in the right direction.

"I see a short man with a funny hat writing in a notebook."

"That's the bookie taking bets. Is there a man next to him? A big, beefy guy?"

"Oh, yes! He's enormous! Tall, huge in every way. The short guy looks like a kid next to him."

"Louis the Gorilla. He owns Platinum Blonde, and she's running today. First time she's run since Lulu was killed. I had hunch he'd be here today, and betting big."

"How do you know people like this?"

"I got around quite a bit in my youth. I kept up with the gentleman of the track. Good way to make a living, if you don't feel like working. But not very dependable. However, if you'd just come into a big pile of money illegally, the racetrack is the only place to do something with it where nobody will ask too many questions. It's especially good if you have a sure bet. I think if you look over at the big board, you'll see the odds dropping on Platinum Blonde."

"You're right. Seven to one, down to three to one."

"Louis must have made a very heavy bet."

"I have a feeling we're going to bet on Platinum Blonde."

"We already have. When the odds were better. It may be the only money I make for solving this case."

A tall, craggy faced cop comes up to Nicky, and he's looking none too happy. Our lost tail, I guess.

"How did you find me, Detective Martin?" Nick asks with a friendly, disarming smile for this flat foot he obviously knows well.

Detective Martin shakes his head in reluctant admiration.

"It wasn't easy. McGirk said you were withholding evidence. So I thought 'Three Fingers...pickpocket....the racetrack...and bingo! I remembered what a fan of the horses you used to be. That was before you, Mrs. Charles," he says, with a respectful smile and nod in my direction. "And I was right. Pretty good, huh, Nick?"

"Top notch, Lieutenant."

"I could run you in for withholding evidence—a bracelet."

Nick pulls it out of his pocket and hands it to Detective Martin.

"This?" The lieutenant looks at it in disbelief. "It's nothing but a cheap piece of junk. What kind of evidence is this?"

"Osberg never took it off. At least, not while he was alive. But whoever killed him thought it was valuable and stole it. I think Lulu used it to blackmail the killer, and he killed her to try to get it back."

The beefy face of the Lieutenant lights up. "Jeeze! So you figure Osberg's dead, too? Could be true, Nick. We've been looking for him for a week and got nothing. Cold trail. But McGirk wouldn't have given you the bracelet, if he did it. He'd have gotten rid of it."

"That's what I figured, Lieutenant. But Lulu was also seeing Louis the Gorilla."

"No kidding. I'll have to go check up on him."

"Here take these binoculars and look over there."

"What!" Detective Martin quickly raises the binoculars to his eyes. "Hey! There he is! I forgot, Louis owns horses." He lowers the binoculars. "Say, I wonder if there's any connection to the jockey who was murdered yesterday. Thanks Nick. I think I'll go over and have a talk with Louis. Afternoon, Mrs. Charles."

"Afternoon, Lieutenant," I reply, as he hot foots it off stage. "Say Nick, how did you know Lulu was blackmailing Louis about killing Osberg?"

"That evidence you got was the key. Eventually it gave me the whole story. McGirk wasn't getting enough money out of Osberg to satisfy Lulu. That was when she got together with Louis. They must have been pushing Osberg pretty hard, because his daughter said her father was going to go to the police about something. Louis must have gotten wind of that. Maybe Osberg threatened him. So he killed him, stripped the body and hid it. When Lulu saw the bracelet, she knew he was dead."

Trumpets blow in the distance. We hear the sound of pounding hooves. Nick shouts, "Look! They're off! Platinum Blonde is in the lead. Go Blondie, go!"

We cheer the horses on together, although no horses are anywhere in the vicinity. That footage, with some added sound effects of pounding hooves, will most likely be put in when the film hits the editing room.

Back in the green room, Alan—if that's his real name. Maybe they do use everyone's real name, it's a reality show, after all. But, I'm not Mrs. Charles. Well, I'll figure this out sooner or later. Meanwhile, Alan is spiffing himself up in front of a full length mirror. How perfect! He's in his sailor whites again; his hat on at a jaunty angle. And he's wearing that mischievous, machismo grin he specializes in.

"Oh, here you are," he says to me. "Been to the racetrack. How civilized."

"And you're still here, too. I thought maybe you'd fallen overboard."

"Only for you, kid. We've got a doozy of a scene coming up. Ready for it?"

"Looking forward to it. I've got a pretty good idea how it goes. You're the hero, the good guy, the action hero who can beat anybody at anything. And me? I'm the bad girl. Naughty girls are smart and fun to play, but they never get the guy, because even action super heroes are no match for a smart girl who knows what she wants. You'll be stuck with the boring, vapid good girl: Lady Missy Prissy."

"Shows how much you know about plot," he scoffs. "You may not be perfect, but you're the leading lady. We've just got to pay our dues before the happy ending. I like you because you *are* smart and know how to get what you want. Me, for instance. And you and I have had some swell times together."

"We did? When did *that* ever happen?"

He puts his arms around my waist and tucks me into his large, manly chest. Encircled by those wide shoulders, we're close enough to kiss. And I can't help thinking that his is the kiss I'd really like to sample.

"When?" he asks in mock outrage. "Why every minute we're together. I've got it so bad for you, I don't know what I'm doing. You're in my blood. Understand? You crazy fool, I want to kiss you so bad."

I wait, lips parted breathlessly, but he just gazes longingly at me.

"Well! So you want to kiss me. Go ahead. I like kissing."

He lets go and puts on his captain's jacket.

"Naw, I'm not gonna get serious about you, because you can't be serious about any guy."

He offers me a cigarette, and we both light up.

"Maybe I don't want you either," I say, after a long, thoughtful drag. "Everybody seems to think I'm in love with you, the big man on the ship, but I don't need you. My character has a career, right?"

"Yeah, sure. You're a night club singer, and you do pretty well in these Asian hot spots. And you've done it all by yourself. Nobody owns you."

"Yeah, yeah! So there!"

He sits down and blows smoke rings. "But you're forgetting—this is a romance."

"Romance," I groan. "Oh no! But it can't be! Not enough heavy breathing, no nudity, no bodice ripping."

"I said *romance*. Love rules here. In a romance, you can be a big success, you know, rich and famous, but still be a loser, because in these stories, love is the gold ring on the merry-go-round, the thing of poet's sonnets and troubadours' ballads."

"My, there's a brain in there."

"Yeah, and speaking of troubadours, wardrobe is waiting for you. You've got work to do."

Indeed I do. It's back to Princess Marion, a true good girl—with a wild streak, judging by the fact she's taken up with Robin Hood, the impudent rascal of Sherwood Forest.

Miss Wardrobe is waiting for me. It's out of the sporty racetrack suit and off with those divine snakeskin pumps and into Maid Marion's royal robes. Even with help, all these costume changes are kind of a nuisance. I vent a little irritation about the unfairness of having to play three roles, while the men are each playing only one.

Without missing a button or zipper, the wardrobe mistress says:

"Take it from Iris, honey, a seasoned veteran of the dating game—forty-five and still can't find the right man, only a lot of the wrong ones—but women always have to play a lot of roles with men. Lover, sister, teacher, mother, best friend, you name it. It's our genius. You got to keep men guessing, or they'll drive you crazy."

Ah, the wisdom of the wardrobe mistress dwarfs anything Nietzsche, Kant, and Simone De Beauvoir have to say— always has, always will.

She finishes my outfit by placing a simple gold band on my head to hold the chiffon snood in place.

"What! No crown? I'm disappointed."

"No, not for this scene. You've escaped from Prince John and run away to Sherwood Forest to warn Robin. You're hoping no one will discover your real identity."

We're shooting outside again on the back lot. This time the crew, director and cameraman are waiting for me a little farther on, deeper amidst the scrub covered hills and tall trees. I look at it all in pleasant amazement, because I had no idea there was so much open land on this lot. Scanning the distant horizon, trying to get my bearings, all I see are more trees and scrub covered hills, which I'm guessing are Griffith Park. Somehow, from where we are I can't see any sign of the Valley, like telephone poles, or buildings or anything. It makes me feel a little strange. How could I not know this was here? I've visited the old Western Town set, which is several blocks of saloons and store front right of a Gary Cooper Western. Maybe we're near that. But I don't have time to worry about it. The camera is ready. I'm shown my focus marks so I don't stray off out of range on the large set. I'm supposed to end up at the entrance to a Tudor Style, thatched roof cottage. Very quaint. Just what you'd expect in this phony, prettified woods. But all right, I'll give it my best shot.

"Roll Camera! Slate! Action!"

I start my walk toward the cottage, determined, brave, and glancing around anxiously to make sure I haven't been followed by any of Prince John's men. In the near distance, I see a tall hooded man approaching. (And so does the camera shooting over my shoulder.) He's coming toward me. Nobody warned me about this guy. He's very big. Could be dangerous. And me without my sword. Rats! Kind of puts me at a slight disadvantage. What's *the girl* supposed to do? Get captured? Scream for help? Run away? Hey, I'm not some sissy princess, I'm Maid Marion. My only weapons are my brain and my wits. If I can't fight this guy, maybe I can outwit him. Being witty is turning out to be more useful that I imagined. Morgan Sidney, bless her cancelled little heart, sometimes found herself in situations where she didn't have her gun, and then she had to outsmart the bad guys. I can do this, and I can do it without a sword.

The hooded man is standing opposite me, and I still can't see his face. He bows slightly and addresses me in a deep toned, soft, yet powerful voice.

"My lady, I don't suppose it's possible that one from your high station in life would know where to find the man I seek. Yet there is no one else to ask."

I hesitate. This could be one of Prince John's tricks.

"Who is the man you seek?"

"He has had some trouble with the law. I'm not sure it's safe to speak his name."

"Perhaps it is the Master of Sherwood Forest."

"And is he the man called Robin Hood?"

"Yes," I answer cautiously. Who is this guy? Why is he hiding his face? "And in Sherwood Forest, no one is safe from him, unless they're loyal to King Richard."

"That is why I'm here alone and unarmed. I seek his protection."

More and more puzzling. But if he's alone and unarmed, what have I got to lose?

"I'm looking for the same man, and it's very urgent. I too was directed to this cottage."

As we knock on the cottage door, a small peep hole is opened and a muffled voice issues from within:

"I would fain ask whom you are inquiring after?"

"We request a meeting with the Master of Sherwood Forest," I say, the total in-charge princess. "I have a message for him. I've risked my life to warn him of danger."

"Good Lady, I don't doubt you. But you, sir, are one of the proud nobility who are the enemies of Robin Hood. What do you want of him?"

"Sir," the hooded man replies. "Can't you see I'm a friar?"

"A rich friar, by the looks of you. Why do you come to Sherwood, where you are sure to be captured and relieved of you heavy purse of gold?"

"I swear I am no threat to Robin Hood."

The door is thrown open to reveal Robin Hood himself.

"Welcome to Sherwood, good friend. I was warned of your approach. Nothing much happens in Sherwood that I do not know about."

"Robin," I exclaim, glad he's in this scene with me. I feel like laughing for the sheer joy of it when he's around. Such a boyishly lively kind of guy, all sinewy grace and wicked smile. "You're in danger Robin! Prince John plans to trap you by staging a tournament. He's awarding a prize to the best archer in the land. But you must not go."

"I am most flattered by you concern, Lady Marion. What is the prize that he has concocted to tempt me?"

"A golden arrow."

"Ah, well," he announces grandly, folding his arms with that incorrigible grin again. "I've no interest in a golden arrow. A gray goose shaft will fly to its mark much truer. John is foolish to think I'd risk my life for so small a prize. Is there nothing else to lure Robin Hood?"

"Ah..." I pause because my cheeks are growing warm, and I can't meet his eyes with my own so full of yearning for another kiss. "A kiss," I mumble to the ground.

"From you, Lady Marion?" He's playing with me, kissing me in every way but the real way. I wish he'd claim that prize right now. "Well, for once Prince John has judged aright. I would certainly risk my life for a kiss from you, fair maid. But, let him try to capture Robin Hood! I will have my men with me, the merry band of Sherwood to capture King John."

Marcy Casterline

"My good man, you speak treason," the hooded friar reacts sharply in outrage, stepping back from us. "John is the legal ruler in his brother's absence."

Provoked and darkly suspicious, Robin replies:

"We shall shortly prove he is not the legal ruler, for he has disobeyed his own laws and left his brother, the rightful and good King, to rot in an Austrian prison awaiting ransom."

With a heavy sigh, the friar responds, "aye, that's true enough. But I hear he has had trouble gathering the ransom."

Anger flashes in Robin's handsome face and his athletic physique seems poised to spring into action. "He's gathered enough from the peasants for ten ransoms, and still Richard is not freed. We are going to raid the treasury and take the ransom to Austria ourselves, if necessary. And you, saucy fellow, I have some doubt of your loyalty to Richard. Can it be we've caught another member of the Church in service to John?"

Robin unsheathes his sword, but the friar doesn't move or respond.

"Speak up man! Or you shall feel the point of my sword. Where do you hail from and what's your business with Robin Hood?"

The hooded friar draws himself erect and slowly throws the hood back, revealing his bearded, and distinguished face.

"I am Richard, King of England." He extends his hand and shows us a king size ring that looks very official as proof.

Robin falls to his knees, and I do the same.

"Your highness! I hope you will overlook my impertinence."

"Nonsense! Robin, you and Lady Marion are my staunchest allies. I was told that Sherwood was the only place I could find safety, and it is true. Now let's gather the men of Sherwood I have a plan to surprise my bother."

"Cut"

Robin walks me back into the building. We chat, and he is just as wild and charming off stage as on. I ask him why he never joins us in the green room, and he tells me he's always practicing his fencing for the big duel with Sir Guy of Gismond when he rescues me from the dungeon. As he trots off to another part of the stage, I think of all the fun things I could do when he rescues me. Faint in his arms, be carried away by him, having his kiss revive me from insensibility and then make me insensible again. Or he could tear me from the clutches of the wicked Sir Guy of Gismond who wants to marry me whether I like it or not. Saved from his clutches as he tries to force himself on me. What thrills are in store for me, all kinds of things no actress gets to do anymore.

Chapter Six

"Hey, what happened to you?" I exclaim as I re-enter the green room from a quick costume change and see Alan looking bruised and dirty. "Where's the smartly turned out Navy Captain we all know and love? I leave you alone for five minutes, while I change into Dolly, the Singapore songstress, and you get all messed up. What happened? A back alley brawl?"

Rubbing a little more stage mud on his face, Alan admires himself in the mirror over the bar.

"Yeah, make-up did a great job. I look terrible. Even got a pretty good shiner, too. Yep! I was in a fight. Got knocked down and beat up. You got me into trouble, Dolly. Girls like you always do."

"I got you into trouble? Well, good for me. So what's next? Is this our big scene?"

"Almost. Now is when we earn those fat paychecks."

He looks me over, appraising my new get up with a wolfishly appreciative glance.

"You sure look swell!"

I sense a note of criticism in his tone. "Of course I look good. I've got a great wardrobe mistress." I spin around in my bias cut, knee-length, flowered chiffon dress with a plunging, ruffled neckline. I've never looked better in my life. There's even a smart, black patent leather belt to accentuate my waist, and the shoes! Open-toed, linen, high heeled pumps and with a guy Alan's height, I can wear high heels and still look girlishly petite—or at least not like Gargantua, the giant girl. I love this dress. It brings out my inner vixen.

"But," Alan says.

"I knew there was a 'but'. What's the matter?"

"Looking good is only half of it. And, well, I'm worried that Louis B. Mayer did the impossible and made a mistake casting you in this part."

"Wasn't Louis B. Mayer the famous dictator producer at MGM, who was never wrong? My, aren't we clever. But I've been doing fine, haven't I?"

"You're okay. But I'm not sure you have what it takes to play your next scene. You're supposed to turn out to be something kind of special. A heroine. Somebody interesting, somebody real."

"What is it about today? Everybody's telling me what I'm not. Maybe *you* don't belong in this picture, either."

He shrugs. "Maybe not. But at least I'm trying. You— you've just been walking through your scenes. Now we'll see what you're made of."

He marches over to the stage door, opens it and with a deep, exaggerated bow, ushers me through. I give him a look of complete disdain, and he laughs, delighted with himself.

We walk out onto the big barn like stage. Across the floor I see a double set, all lit and furnished for action. On one side, it's the ship's bar again. The other set is the bridge of the ship, with the classic wood spoked steering wheel, a table for maps, and a stool and some chairs. They have two cameras set up, one on each set. I guess they're going to film two scenes in real time. The action overlaps, and it's probably easier and more spontaneous to do it this way.

I stride confidently toward the director, wondering which set is for me. My dress flutters around my legs flirtatiously. Given that this is going to be a demanding scene, I hope the director will condescend to give me some help.

Smiling for all I'm worth, I catch his eye. He smiles back, points to the far set and says, "you're in the bar." Then he goes right back to a conference with his two cameramen, setting up the shots. Oh well, most directors are like that, more concerned with technical things than the acting.

The stage manager helps me through the forest of lights, cables and gear onto my set. I see Alan, with dirty face and torn uniform, head onto the ship's bridge set. I sit down at my usual table and help myself to a drink. What else is there to do at a bar?

"Action!"

Oh boy! Here we go. The stage reverberates with gunfire, shouts, and screams. It's all very real. Jamesie bursts into the bar, his face alive with excitement, and his eyes gleaming.

"The pirates have attacked! They're rounding up the passengers in the ballroom. We'll have the gold soon. And we'll be rich, Dolly, rich!" He's practically frothing at the mouth with anticipation.

He pours himself a shot and downs it. Then he leers at me. (Bernie, you dirty old man, I didn't know you had it in you.)

"I couldn't have done it without my little songbird," he purrs. "You got me the key to the ship's arsenal, so I could arm the pirates. Without their guns, the crew didn't stand a chance of stopping the attack." Jamesie pats my cheek fondly.

"Oh, right, the key," I remember it well. It was the key or get strangled.

As the gunshots and screaming continue, with the sound of furniture crashing around on the other set adding to the mayhem, I throw down another drink.

"Jamesie, you said no one would be hurt."

"Don't worry about that, it's their own fault for resisting. I hope Alan is smart and tells them where the gold is hidden, otherwise..."

"Otherwise what?" I ask, as a chill of fear runs down my spine.

From the second set, the ship's bridge, which I can't see but can hear plainly enough (and I guess I'm supposed to be able to hear) there are loud scuffling noises. Suddenly Alan shouts:

"Let go of me, you filthy pirates! How'd you get those guns? They're the ships guns. How'd you get the key? Dammit!"

More furious scuffling. They must be fighting. I gulp. How am I supposed to be the heroine? I stole the key and gave it to Jamesie when he caught me trying to warn Alan. Hey, is it my fault Alan wouldn't listen, and I got caught and had to save my own skin?

Jamesie's back on the other set.

"Alan, I just want to help you," Jamesie coos, all full of concern, like he's Alan's best friend. "I speak Malay. They just want to know where the safe with the gold is. You'd better tell them. These pirates do terrible things to people."

Alan barks his answer like he's still in command of the ship. "Untie me! Jamesie, tell them there is no gold. It's on another ship. They've got the wrong ship."

"They don't believe you. Oh no! It's the Malay boot! Oh, Captain, I can't stand it."

"Well look the other way," Alan snarls and then groans loudly.

"He's fainted from the pain. Throw a bucket of water over him," Jamesie orders impatiently. "We'll get him to talk."

I hear the water splash. Then they slap Alan to bring him moaning and cursing back to consciousness. He pleads weakly with Jamesie.

"It's on the other ship. Jamesie, tell them to leave me alone. Oh no! Not again! I can't stand it."

There's a bloodcurdling cry, then a moan followed by silence. I can't stand it either. They must be torturing him with the Malay boot. Whatever that is, sounds like it really hurts. I pace around the bar, trying to think. But what can I do? They didn't give me a gun. I don't know karate. Wit would be useless on Pirates who don't speak English. Maybe I have super powers. Oh forget that! I don't want to be a comic book heroine.

With an ugly look on his face, Jamesie slams back into the bar, grabs a bottle, sits down and pours himself a stiff one. I join him at the table.

"He won't talk. He's fainted from the boot. The pirates are combing the ship. They'll find that gold, don't you worry."

"They're torturing him, Jamesie. Are they going to kill him?"

"Oh, you can never tell what these pirates will do."

I slump in my chair, full of despair. "I wish I'd never gotten involved in this."

"Aw don't get so upset. Captain Gaskell struts around, acting so high and mighty. But he won't strut so much after the Malay boot."

"What do you mean?"

"It breaks every bone in your foot. He won't ever walk right again."

Horrified, I hide my face in my hands. What did I help do?

"Dolly, listen to me," Jamesie pulls my hands from my face. "Did Alan ever mention anything about a safe? Or bank deposits? Or gold? Think Dolly!"

Believe me, I am thinking. I could say he told me there was no gold, but Jamesie would see right through that. I seem to be a total failure at the heroine job. If this is reality TV, nobody will vote for me.

"No, no, he never said a word about anything like that. Are you sure it's on the ship?"

"Of course I'm sure. I've got spies all over the waterfront. He's hidden it somewhere, that's all. If we can't find it, the boot'll get it out of him, don't you worry."

Jamesie exits my set and goes back to the bridge with renewed determination to get the gold. Obviously, they're going to torture Alan again. Jamesie is in cahoots with the pirates, and because I got too friendly with my old pal, so am I. Can I help it if Dolly drives men wild? Anybody with a name like Dolly was bound to drive men wild. But what am I supposed to do? Seduce the pirates? Don't think that would work, unless Johnny Depp is one of them. Morgan Sidney always knew what to do. But of course with a name like Morgan, you knew she was tough, sensible. She wouldn't have gotten mixed up with Jamesie to begin with. Being a detective had its limitations, though—more business, less flirting. But what can I do? Feel happy Alan is getting what he deserves for insulting me instead of listening to me? But I'm in trouble, because other people have been hurt, too. Am I supposed to be in love with Alan? That seems to be the general idea—in love and rejected. I can hear the stupid camera still rolling. What do they want from me? Maybe I am miscast. I throw down a phony shot of scotch in disgust, wishing it was the real thing.

"He's come to," I hear Jamesie say on the bridge set. "Oh, Alan," he pleads, all smarmy nice again. "Tell them, Alan. They know you're carrying a big shipment of deposits for the bank. It's terrible what they're doing to you. You can't take it anymore."

Sounding totally wiped out, Alan says, "Stop trying to cheer me up. Tell them there is no gold."

He groans loudly, and it's painful to hear.

"Aw, he's fainted again. He'd have talked by now. Nobody can stand the boot. There's no money!"

I hear a lot of pirate chatter in a foreign language, then Jamesie says:

"You sure you looked everywhere? All right, you thieving wretches, get out of here. You've robbed the passengers, that'll have to do."

"Cut!"

On the way back to the green room, everyone is loading up plates of Chinese food. Someone ran over to the Formosa Café and got it for the cast and crew. I'm starved and so is everyone else. We all load up our plates.

When Alan sits down to eat, the make-up man props his foot up on a stool and begins wrapping it in thick, white bandages. I sit down opposite him, and as soon as he sees me, his face lights up.

"You were great, kid. You played that scene just right. No mushy, sentimental overacting. Dolly had real dignity. She didn't just cry and feel sorry for herself."

"You mean it? I thought I stank up the screen. So I was okay." I breathe a sigh of relief. Kind of nice to play a character who isn't perfect. "That was awful that Malay boot torture. You're a pretty courageous Captain. But do you have the money or what?"

"Yeah, but it's well hidden."

"Why not just give it to the pirates? What's so important about some gold?"

He stops eating and stares at me like he can't believe what I just said.

"It's the Captain's job to deliver that money safely. If it fell into the hands of the pirates, they'd have more money to buy guns and build up their operations to rob and pillage more innocent people. Besides, that money represents the savings of lots of hardworking people. It's my job, and I do it. That's all."

"That's impressive. Something money can't buy. Not many people around like that."

"Aw sure there are. Lotsa people do the right thing. They may not get the Malay boot, but there are plenty of things in life just as tough to put up with."

"Still, your character did the right thing, and mine didn't. I guess I am kind of a flawed character."

He puts his empty plate aside.

"Don't get all carried away about it. Remember, I'm also short-tempered, impatient, glum and bossy. I drink too much and complain a lot. And, I'm about to quit all this for the classy dame and go back to England, far away from this messy life."

"Yeah, yeah," I dismiss all this masculine condescension, this trying to make me feel not as bad as I do. "But you've proved you deserve the classy dame. Really. Go ahead, dump my character. She's a screw-up."

"Gee thanks," he replies sarcastically. "You still don't get it about romance, do you?"

"But this isn't romance, not strictly speaking, is it? If this was real honest-to-god romance, you'd be better looking for starters. I mean, you're attractive, but hardly romance hero perfect. Sorry."

"I'll never be able to look at myself in the mirror again," he responds lightly.

"Aw, come on, you know what I mean." What a wise guy. He's begging for a fight. Well, I'm just the girl to give it to him. "You're not rich, never will be, and being a Captain is really kind of a blue collar job, isn't it?"

"What's your point? A working class stiff not good enough for a dame like you?"

"I just can't see why my character would ever consider exchanging her freedom and future for a guy like you. You can't give me anything that I can't get for myself."

"Why would I want to burden myself with you, for that matter? I work and pay the bills, and you raise the kids. What more do you want?"

"A career," I announce triumphantly, well schooled in the feminist dialectic. But he's not impressed. In fact, he laughs in my face like I'm crazy.

"A career!" he howls. "Isn't it bad enough that one of us has to go out and take all the guff the world has to offer?"

"But you'll be having all the fun, getting all the glory, while I change diapers."

"Oh, lots of fun and glory. I'll have all the rewards a job can give—five percent success, ninety-five percent sweat, frustration, and disappointment. You know I'm right. You work now. How often does your job make you feel great?"

A Rogue, A Pirate, and A Dry Martini

"Well, you've got a point, but today has been fun." Still, most days are just work. Memories of the long shooting days on *Morgan Sidney* crowd my mind. It was often boring, repetitive, and tedious, like any job, I guess. "But who would I be if I wasn't working?" I fling back to challenge his complacency.

Alan fixes my eyes with a steady gaze, as he replies, "My wife, for instance—a mother, for instance. The person who creates a happy home and with my help raises our kids and turns them into decent, happy people. And you can sing in church on Sundays, if you still need an audience. Ever been?"

"To Church? No."

"You might like it."

We stare at each other across miles of distrust. This guy is a challenge. I'll give him that.

"Okay," I say. "I give up everything. And how do I know you'll stick with me?"

He kicks back in his chair, cocky, confident Mr. Know-it-all. "There are no guarantees in life. You're on your own. You have to make the judgment call. Am I the guy who'll mean what he says? Am I the guy who'll keep his promises?"

"In sickness and in health, for better or for worse, tell death do us part. Yeah right."

He says in a low, quiet voice, "I gotta think about that, too."

"You do that." I rise to go change my costume. "Oh, by the way, let me know when the story gets romantic."

"What makes you think you deserve romance?" he calls after me. "I'm not too fond of you right now. Observe." He lifts his thickly bandaged foot for me to take note of.

"Oh, yeah, I forgot. I guess you wouldn't feel too romantic about me. But I bet I could get you all hot and bothered if I want to."

I strike a seductive pose and undulate through a few moves at the door to my dressing room. I've got a good figure and know how to use it. And in my flirty dress, I'm total man bait. He's looking at me and can't help smiling. I got him. He wants me. But with a guy like him, is that enough?

"I guess we'll see in the next scene or two" he comments lighting a cigarette and looking as if he relished the prospect of finding out.

Chapter Seven

The door to the green room flies open, and Robin lunges in with his sword drawn, shadow fencing all around the room. Robin Hood is always there when you need him, ready to do your bidding, if you're a princess. Now he really is the perfect romantic leading man. But even *he* is different, somehow, a far cry from the usual vapid, preening, vain heroes in big epic pictures I've seen recently.

"Get into costume, my lady. My big dueling scene is next. The one where I rescue you from John, and we storm the castle."

I roll my eyes, grab a half empty martini glass from the bar and throw down the contents, wondering how much more of his boyish exuberance I can stand.

"Okay, okay. Give me a minute."

After a quick change, I'm back to being a crowned head of Europe and following Robin to a new stage set. It's an enormous castle interior, at least three stories high. A stone staircase spirals upward, around a turret. There's a giant fireplace so big I could stand in it. But no fire at the moment. I guess they're going to burn me later. Hah hah.

Another very good looking man, tall, distinguished and in appropriate medieval garb, mail shirt, tunic, sword in hand, is waiting on the set, slashing the air with his sword, lunging and feinting in mock battle. He pauses to introduce himself to me with exquisite politeness, (I don't recognize his name) and tells me that he plays Sir Guy of Gismond, my intended groom, the man who wants me, but wants to kill Robin more.

Then he and Robin laugh together and cut up a little to relieve the tension and excitement. When it's time to shoot, they position me at the bottom of the stairs. And it's:

"Action!"

And this time it's really action. At the head of the stairs, Robin is coming down backwards, fighting all the way. The two really go at it. They're good. Obviously well rehearsed.

"Robin Hood!" Sir Guy exclaims "On garde, you slimy cur! I've been looking forward to this moment for a long time."

"I'm afraid it will be a short match, Sir Guy, just as long as it takes to part your liver from your spleen."

I watch Robin creep backwards down the spiral stairs, with Sir Guy bearing down on him. Then Robin moves in on Sir Guy, then Sir Guy recovers and pins Robin against the wall. This is never my favorite part of any movie. I'm just not interested in the fighting; not with swords, fists, or karate, not even if they can fly, like in the Chinese karate films. Mostly these scenes seem interminable. All I need to know is who wins.

But I must say, in spite of my prejudices, I am enjoying this duel. Both of these guys look great, dancing gracefully around the room, in an elegant, but deadly battle.

Robin actually does seem in danger of losing. Sir Guy of Gismond is quite adept with his sword. They are moving so quickly back and forth across the set, I decide it's best just to stay where I am flattened against the faux stone staircase, doing the worried female act. It's what you have to do to earn the kiss.

A Rogue, A Pirate, and A Dry Martini

My mind wanders, as the two of them upend a chair on the opposite side of the set. Since I can see I'm not in the shot at the moment, I glance off stage and watch the big old camera being cranked up higher for a better angle on the action. They seem to be doing the fight all in one take, seamless, no cuts. The guys in the audience will love that.

All of the crew are performing their duties with precision, all of which I'm only too familiar with: the sound man holding the boom mike aloft; the director of photography zooming the focus in and out; and the grips pushing the camera dolly across the floor for a long, smooth tracking shot. It all looks very well rehearsed.

And that doesn't really make sense. Something's not right about this. Everyone is perfectly serious, doing his or her jobs flawlessly. But how could I be doing mine? Who was supposed to be playing 'the girl'? Where is she? Why don't they care? I can't figure this all out, and it makes me feel funny, sort of discombobulated.

Suddenly Sir Guy is stabbed; he goes down, falling to the ground with a last few curses at Robin.

"Cut"

The crew applauds the actors fine sword play. Sir Guy rises, and he and Robin take their bows and applaud the crew for the fancy camera work.

Thank God that's over. I head back to the green room, still feeling a little dizzy and confused. Alan is there alone, lounging around looking very comfortable.

I collapse into one of the commodious old armchairs, pulling the crown and snood off my head. The crown makes my head ache. I massage my temples and lay back with my eyes closed, sighing gigantically.

"You all right?" Alan asks sympathetically.

"I guess so. Probably just tired. Boy, am I ever having trouble motivating the Robin Hood stuff. It's all so high flown and noble. And it's all way too pretty to be real. I mean it would help if they got some of the details right, like the peasants. They should be filthy, like real twelfth century peasants. And Robin in those ridiculous tights. I know they wore hose in those days, but it probably sagged and was full of holes. His tights are so perfect. I love them, but...come on, really shouldn't the merry men of Sherwood be coarse and toothless and burping? You know, taking a piss in the forest like real life."

Is it pity or incredulity or both that I see in Alan's eyes before he laughs with delight, sitting up and shaking his head? "Yeah, yeah, I can see it all now, the merry old farts of England," he throws his head back, laughing helplessly. "You're so funny; I haven't laughed this hard in years."

This is not at all the response I was looking for.

"No, now stop it." I insist. "I'm being serious. And these movies, or whatever they are, would be more serious if they were more real. Every really good film these days has to have a pissing scene. It's part of life."

"Cut it out," he's bursts into laughter again. "You're killing me."

"What's so funny? I don't get it?"

He stares at me, like he isn't sure I'm kidding or not. Then he starts laughing again, even harder now. "Stop! Stop! People paying good money, lining up at the box office to see peasants pissing and farting, and not just any peasants, they have to be dirty peasants." He's laughing again almost uncontrollably, and it's contagious. I even start to chuckle at the idea of people paying to watch other people piss, even though every movie I've gone to for the last ten years has a piss scene. And I laugh even harder when I realize that the only place I ever do watch other people piss is in the movies. I mean, where else? So how is that more real life? How stupid!

When we're both laughed out, I feel much better. Dizziness gone. Thinking straight again.

"So Alan, we're alone here. Give me a heads up. What's going on? You were expecting me today, weren't you?"

"Sure."

"Who set this all up?"

He gives me a quizzical glance. "I don't know what you're driving at, but I'll play along. Your agent set this up. Just like mine did."

"Then this is some kind of improv thing, right?"

"We try to create a certain spontaneity. Yes, true."

"And will they use all these little vignettes to make a gag reel, or something like that?"

"If you want to call it that. But when we're finished shooting, there will be a whole film."

"Finished shooting? What do you mean?"

"We're back tomorrow and for about another four weeks of shooting."

"We are? And my agent set this up? But what do they do with these films?"

"What everybody does with films." He looks at me like I've lost my mind. "Send 'em off to movie theaters around the country. Are you all right?"

I jerk bolt upright in my chair. "Oh God no! You can't show these in theaters. It'll ruin my career. I thought this was a stunt, a gag, a one shot deal for a reality show. I look like an idiot. I wasn't really trying to act, I was just having fun."

Marcy Casterline

"They say that's the key to great film acting."

"No, no, you can't do this to me. It really, *really* will end my career. I can't be seen in stuff like this. No one will ever take me seriously again."

I sink back into the depths of my chair in total despair. I'm ruined. Totally ruined. Why did Bernie get me involved in this? He should have asked me, spoken to me, before getting me into some experimental film like this. He *knows* I'd turn something like this down. A light bulb in the brain. That's why he didn't tell me. Because he didn't want to give me the chance to turn it down. It's my last hope—all he could get for me. Horrors! But wait. Bernie's doing it too. I never knew he had acting ambitions, and he's pretty good. But he's a complete unknown, as are all these guys, so they have no careers to ruin. Oh bummer! Why did I ever get up this morning?

Nick enters, notes my gloomy condition, makes martinis and hands them around.

"What's the matter?" he inquires innocently.

Alan responds, "I think she's a little tired. You know, she's worried about her career and her performance."

"Aah," Nick exhales sagely. "Everyone goes through that sometimes. Drink up. You'll get over it."

I sip the martini in a total state of panic. "Listen, I can't go on with this. This stuff just isn't me. It's ridiculous! A ship in a typhoon! Merrie Olde England!"

"No typhoons or sword fights in our story," Nicky points out.

"No, but everything else was extremely improbable. For instance, the cast of overwrought lowlifes with silly names who are all having affairs and robbing each other. Who wants to see a movie like that? It's irrelevant and unrealistic." I'm devastated, as only a person in show biz can be devastated, where one tiny mistake can cost you your career. "A third rate ship's captain? A tipsy detective? A rebel who lives in the woods? This stuff is awful! Tripe! Unimportant drivel."

They both stare at me for a long uncomfortable moment. I know I've hurt their feelings, but maybe it's better if we all face the truth about what we're working on here. Nick heads for the bar.

"I'd better make another round of drinks."

"You drink too much," I snap at him. Nevertheless, I down my first martini and start on the second. Why not? My life is so over.

Nick seats himself comfortably in a wing chair, sips his drink and fixes me with his unflinching, but gentle gaze.

"Yes, I enjoy my drinks. Maybe I drink more than I should, but I am first and foremost a discreet man. I never drink so much that it interferes with my life or anyone else's. And this 'tipsy detective' has solved quite a number of murder cases where things would have gone quite another way had I not been involved. I use my knowledge of what you call lowlifes, because I know people from all walks of life. I've taken the time and trouble to know them and be interested in their lives, and occasionally help them. It's not steady work. I'm far from rich. But through life's twists and turns..."

"You're a survivor," I sneer.

"Excuse me. I aim a little higher than that. I feel I've achieved a certain sophistication, which helps me make it through life's up and downs, without snobbery or hypocrisy, and remain a gentleman. I have my dignity, and I don't rob others of theirs. Pardon me, if I'm a little proud of my achievements and resent having my work referred to as drivel. Now drink your martini and try to regain your senses."

"Okay, okay. I'm sorry if I offended you. But come on, typhoons? Pirates? These films are nothing but cheap, escapist entertainment, light weight junk for the drooling, illiterate masses."

Alan casually flicks the ash off his cigarette. "Is this my cue?"

"Yeah," I reply belligerently. "How many typhoons have you been in?"

"More than you might imagine. My real life would probably surprise you. But you're missing the point."

"Oh, sure, I know. This stuff gets people minds off their problems. But face it, it's fluff—at best."

Alan sits up, rousing himself to a vertical position, his face suddenly serious, his eyes burning with passion.

"That's where you're wrong. These movies are full of information about how to live better, or people wouldn't shell out good money for them."

"Right," I wave my hand dismissively, "information like watch out for pirates, if you happen to find yourself traveling by ship in the Far East." I roll my eyes dramatically, hoping to make it clear that he's not going to get away with any half-baked nonsense around me, no sir. I'm going to be this poor, second-rate actor's slap of cold water and save him from wasting any more of his time in show business.

Alan is on his feet, all coiled virility and anger, moving toward me like a panther. We're eye to eye, practically a stare down contest. He starts on me:

"Haven't you ever run into a pirate? Somebody who snuck up on you, when you were looking the other way, and took something from you that you needed badly and had to get along without, when they were finished with you? Who used you, and maybe a big piece of your life was never the same again."

"Yes, sort of." I draw a quick breath, because I do see what he's saying, and I know I have been in that situation. My dear producer, ex-boyfriend, Justin, stole part of my life, while I was trying to grow up and do my job and get somewhere. I guess he qualifies as a pirate of sorts.

Alan's eyes bore into me. "I don't believe it. I think it's all been easy for you. You've never had to try hard, to struggle to survive. You've got a pretty face and a certain facility as an actress, but I don't see any compassion in those eyes. Well, everybody's not as lucky as you. Some of us have woken up in the morning broke, hungry, without hope, and running out of time. That's what these movies are about. Emotional truths. Metaphorical truths. Do you know what that means?"

My own words, my own conceit, thrown back in my face. "Yes," I answer stiffly, a little ashamed of myself. He's right. Yeah, I've been working since I was a kid, but we were never broke, never hungry. He's nailed me to a T.

He lights a cigarette and hands it to me, then one for himself.

"Good. Sit down." I do, very erect. "The typhoon is a metaphor for how it feels to have the wind knocked out of you by life. The way some people help, and some make it worse. If they're good enough, these movies make you believe that even if all you have is gumption, humor and generosity, you can make it. And people need to feel that so badly that they line up around the block to go to the movies. Do you think you can motivate yourself now?"

He returns to the sofa, sits back down and finishes his cigarette.

I gather my wits and catch my breath, taking a moment to consider what he's said. I like it. I like him for feeling so passionately about his job. Poor fool. I hate to wise up such noble innocence; although he actually doesn't seem innocent or naive—no way. But I know what people line up around the block for—raunchy sex, raunchy violence, raunchy humor, car crashes, gunfights, and computer-generated graphics by the truckload, nothing noble about it. No one in a million trillion years would ever line up for, let alone watch any of these films we're making.

"Metaphors," I say, ready to make peace. "So these sort of over-the-top, sentimental, mushy romance stories are actually metaphors. But I hate to tell you, most men are not like you. Most men don't take romance seriously. Macho guys—although you do seem pretty macho—but in general, macho guys scorn this kind of film. Frankly, the stuff we're shooting here wouldn't even make it on the Women's channel." Then, with a sad shake of my head, I add, "romance, phooey!"

As if on cue, Robin enters, looks around and leaps onto a table, slashing the air with his sword.

"To Romance! To Truth! Honor! Beauty! To Richard The Lionheart! Drinks for my thirsty companions, and hay for my horses. Lady Marion, I'll be back to claim your hand in marriage."

He jumps down, lunges around and raising his sword to his forehead, bows deeply to me. "I hope you'll be ready when I return."

He exits to our general relief, although Nick and Alan don't seem as surprised or bothered as I am.

"What enthusiasm!" I comment sarcastically, then to Alan, "and I thought you had overactive hormones."

Alan rises effortlessly to his feet and off-handedly, almost hopelessly, adds, "it's love. Romance is about love. Now if you'll excuse me, I have to get into my dress whites for our last scene."

Nick excuses himself and goes to his dressing room.

I stand up too. I'm sure I should go to my dressing room and change, but I'm not satisfied. I feel frustrated and confused by what we're doing here. I just can't get enthusiastic about it, can't commit myself to it. It's really difficult to do emotional scenes when you feel all wishy-washy like this. I've got to have some answers, before I go on. So I follow Alan to his dressing room, pausing at the door politely. He takes off his jacket and throws it on the chair.

"Love?" I say thoughtfully, and, I suppose, leadingly. "Don't tell me you believe in love."

His dressing room is the same size as mine. Not posh satin like mine, but comfortable, with the same bare bulbs framing a vanity mirror, and a rack of freshly pressed white linen naval uniforms. He glances at me, before sitting down in front of the mirror. Without replying, he starts to trim his moustache. But he hasn't asked me to leave, and that's invitation enough. So I begin, leaning against the doorframe, with my arms crossed:

"Oh brother, let me tell you about love. It has a lot to do with a good time slot."

"Is that so?" he replies absently.

"Yeah." A sad little sigh escapes me. Nothing like an almost complete stranger to unburden your soul to. "What is it they say, 'when you're hot, you're hot, and when you're not, you're not'. I don't want to burst your bubble, but careerwise, we're not hot."

Unbuttoning his shirt, without so much as a glance in my direction, he replies, "are you hot? I am."

He stands up, loosens his shirttails from his pants, undoes his shirt cuffs and strips it off. Bare-chested, he's quite the delectable stud. A little hair on the chest. His muscles are lean and sinewy, and I'm not at all sorry I followed him.

"Your type is always hot," I say uneasily. Well it's sort of a compliment, the best I can do at the moment.

Throwing me a coy look, not to be bested in the smart remark contest, he parries with, "what type is that? The masculine type? But you see, that's where I'm different. Most men go for the pants next, but I'm the delicate type, oh my, yes. I don't bother with the pants, until I'm in love."

I stare at him, challenging him to go for the pants. "Love? Is that really what gets men to drop trouser? Give me a break! Love is a con job."

"If that's the way you feel, you'd better go to your own dressing room, because I'm not easy. Oh, my no! I was brought up to think better of myself. Now don't trifle with me. Women like you are the reason I go for the shoes next."

His smile is smug and cold, as he raises a foot to the chair and begins to untie his shoe.

"If you want to call it love, go ahead, big guy, but you won't fool me or any smart girl. It's all just biology. Nothing sweet or wonderful or delicate about it."

He's on the other shoe. Watch out.

"Is that so? You actually think this crazy mixed up world would have gotten as far as it has without love?" he says, removing a sock.

"Trust me, Love had nothing to do with it. It's just a primordial urge. Eating and screwing make the world go round."

He straightens up, fists on hips, staring me down. I'm breathing hard. Half naked, muscular men do that to a girl. He doesn't need to do more than take his shirt off. Wow. Talk about your primordial urge. I've got it bad for this guy.

"Well," he says, matter-of-factly, "Romance pictures are nothing without love. Without love, there would be no happy endings. But play it your way, and we'll see what happens."

He doesn't take his eyes off me. His hands are on his belt buckle. "It's every man for himself, if you know what I mean."

Blushing furiously, I beat a hasty retreat to my dressing room. Much too hasty for a grown-up woman who's seen it all. What's the matter with me? Why run away when I was about to get just what I wanted? Because I can't figure this guy out, and that scares me.

Iris is waiting for me with my tweed sports suit and snakeskin sling backs.

"Back to the racetrack?"

"Yeah."

"Tell me about Alan. What's the story with him?"

"Well, honey," Iris replies as briskly as she tells you to button up your blouse. "The short answer is stay away. He's catnip for women. Guaranteed heart breaker. Girls fall for him like ninepins in a bowling alley. He may not be hard to get, but he's hard to keep. So consider yourself warned."

"Thanks," I reply, slightly taken aback by the finality of her verdict.

A hairdresser enters, and Iris introduces her as Dorothy. She's slim, in her forties with bangs and a chin length bob, very chic. She's got a huge bag of hair styling gear, which she throws on the floor by the dressing table.

Taking out an old fashioned curling iron, the kind all hair stylists use, because they're hot and fast, she plugs it in and goes to work on my hair as I sit in front of the mirror. Having you hair done is always relaxing and very conducive to intimate conversation. Iris is nearby ironing some wrinkles out of my blouse.

Dreamily, I ask, "Iris, so tell me, do you *like* Alan?"

She looks up from her iron. "That's the worst part about him. You can't help liking him."

"Well, I don't have to worry. I'm not coming back tomorrow. They'll have to get some other girl. This kind of work will ruin my career."

Iris spits on the iron to test the heat. "Oh great. You hear that Dorothy? We've got another temperamental star on our hands. Listen, smarty pants, if you get the studio bosses mad at you, you won't have a career to worry about."

This is only too true. "But, Iris, I can't believe they're going to release these films. No one will come to see them."

Iris snickers. Wardrobe people and hairdressers have seen it all and never let you forget it. And that's usually a good thing. Often the real drama, the sturm und drang, is in the dressing room, not on the set.

A Rogue, A Pirate, and A Dry Martini

"I've seen them come, and I've seen them go. And there are lots of actresses out there looking for a job, just like you are. You'll be back."

Shit. It's already around the whole lot that I've been cancelled. Humbling.

"Yeah, I guess I will."

I play with my make-up, doing a sort of thirties style look to go with the clothes. I make my face pale, arch the brows, dark matte lipstick, and blush to deepen the cheek hollows.

Dorothy is pulling on my hair, wrapping it tightly in the curling iron.

"Don't let Iris get to you, honey," she says with an impish grin on her highly rouged face. "She's always jealous of anyone who gets to work with Alan. She's stuck on him and wants him all for herself. Don't you, Iris?"

The hard-boiled wardrobe mistress vanishes, and Iris smiles girlishly and blushes. She's thrilled to be teased about Alan. If she really likes him, he can't be so bad.

"Oh go on, Dorothy. He doesn't even notice me."

"He calls you his best girl and hugs you, doesn't he?'

A deeper blush spreads over Iris's face. She keeps her head down, her eyes fixed on her ironing. "If I were younger. But he knows I just want to see him settle down. At the rate he's going, he won't make forty. Partying every night with a different girl. He needs a good woman to keep him home at night. But the bad girls won't let him alone."

The conversation then veers off in another direction about the love lives of people I've never heard of. Dorothy lights a cigarette and hands it to me, while she finishes off my hair. Guess there are no anticigarette Nazis on this set. And she's actually doing a great job on my hair. It's all loose and fluffy and very feminine. Well, at least I'll look good.

Chapter Eight

Back in the green room, Nick is waiting for me. He's wearing a shoulder holster, as he shakes up the martinis. I'm definitely going to have to cab it home tonight. No driving after all these martinis. He puts his jacket on and adjusts a handkerchief in his breast pocket, pulling points up smartly. He's one sharp dresser.

Alan ambles in casually, giving me a brief smile that's too confident by half and makes me think he's up to something. He's all dressed up in a clean new captain's uniform.

Nick hands me a short martini, as he says, "this next scene is tough. So have a sip and relax. You've got to be mad and dangerous."

"Sounds like fun."

"This is where you steal the show, and I and the audience love you for it."

"I do? They do?"

Nick smiles at me. "Of course. And you look marvelous."

But Alan won't let me feel good for a second.

"Yeah," he says, really enjoying this. "You LOVE Nick so much you do something crazy. Do you think you can motivate that?"

"I'm sure I can. I believe in love, to a point."

"I guess we'll find out just where that point is," Alan responds coolly.

"Please don't make the lady nervous. We want to get this in one take. A person can't be mad and dangerous twice in one day."

Then Nick leads me out of the green room, with a protective arm around my waist and a reproachful backward glance at Alan. But Alan is undaunted, or perhaps just curious, and follows us to the set.

"You don't mind if I watch, do you? I want to see what mad dangerous love looks like," he says, finding this all just hilarious.

The set is an ordinary, somewhat shabby office interior. It's been lit to look like it's night, but with enough light so the players can be seen. Open Venetian blinds let fake streetlight pour into the room in film noire shadowy stripes across the desks and file cabinets. Louis The Gorilla is already on the set and seems to take up half the room. Two other guys are tied and gagged in wooden office chairs.

Giving me a peck on the cheek, Nick says, "I'll be waiting for you." Then he joins Louis on the set.

Alan, standing right beside me, whispers in my ear, "and waiting and waiting..."

Nick takes his place center stage, lit dramatically with a key light to make sure the camera captures every glint of intelligence in his eyes, and every fleeting emotion to cross his face.

Suave, as always, Nick begins after the director calls "Action!"

"Louis, I'm sorry to surprise you in your office at this hour. You're not going to like this, but somebody's been fixing the races at the track. And I have proof that these two commissioners I've detained here are on the take. Somehow, "Platinum Blonde" wins whenever Shorty rides her. I wonder if it was you, Louis, who's been using the money you and Lulu stole to fix these races and win big. Quite a scheme," Nick says with an off-handed flourish. He's one of those rare actors who make it look so easy. Sad really, no one cares about acting anymore. It's all stunts and special effects and computer cartoons. This is probably the only job he can get or will ever have.

"That's enough, Nick," Louis growls, hurling his massive bulk at Nick.

Nick goes for his gun. There's an incredibly realistic scuffle between them. But the Gorilla prevails, grabbing Nick's gun and pointing it at him.

"Now you're all gonna die. I'm gonna shoot you first, Nick, then Malone and Peters. The cops will think they killed you because you caught them paying off the jockeys. And they'll be killed in the shootout with your own gun. And that'll take care of all of you."

The director calls "Cut" and the make-up people rush in, pat the drenching sweat off Louis's face. He's perspired so much in the fight scene that his pancake make-up is streaking down his face.

While everyone holds their places to continue, Alan whispers to me, "your cue is coming up."

My eyes go wide in panic. Mad and dangerous! I don't think that's my strong suit as an actress.

"What am I supposed to do? I don't have a gun or anything."

"You're supposed to race in and throw yourself on Louis and in front of the gun, shouting 'Run, Nicky, Run!' You're going to look awfully silly trying to do that for biological reasons. Can you do it?"

I frantically study the set up, trying to think of an alternative plan, not to mention something better to say than 'run, Nicky, run'; but I come up with nothing.

"You're right. I don't know if I can motivate that. I mean why would I, or anyone, do that? Besides, Nick can take care of himself."

Alan folds his arms, grinning at me triumphantly.

"Fraid not. Not this time. He needs your help. That guy can shoot him, and the other two bodies will make a real convincing story. And don't forget, Nick Charles won't be around to investigate and find out the real story."

"But the Gorilla will shoot *me*!"

"Maybe. Maybe you'll buy Nick enough time to do something."

Morgan Sidney rescued plenty of people, but she always had a gun, or a plan or a cop or something to outsmart the bad guy.

"You're chicken. You're afraid of love. You don't belong in a romance. Romance isn't for cowards."

"Dammit! I'm not a coward."

"Well, then let's see you do it. 'Run, Nicky Run'. Don't you want to save him? He's been pretty swell to you."

I'm sweating, wringing my hands, caught in a trap. "Yeah, he has."

"Not many guys around like Nick. He's no saint, but he's an original."

"I like him. He's sophisticated. We had some fun together." (Wow, I'm breathing fast. I'm pushing myself hard to get my emotions up to ramming speed.) "He took a bullet for me—well, it grazed him. And he's a great kisser."

"He loves you."

"Oh! That word again!" I deflate like a balloon. I couldn't save anyone from anything now. "Listen you big nosey beefcake, I feel really stupid. It's just so over-emotional."

"You're going to have to do something, or Nick Charles will be a goner."

"Stop pushing me! He *is* such a great guy. And he does make a killer martini. But this is the stupidest movie. Who wrote this crap? 'Run, Nicky, Run'. I can't say that. I'll say 'watch out Nick'."

Alan laughs delightedly, and I could kill him.

Louis is all fixed up and everyone on set is ready. My mouth is as dry as cotton, when the director calls "Action!"

"Nick," the Gorilla says, assuming his former position, holding a gun on Nick. "I've been looking forward to this for years. Your death will solve a lot of my problems."

Louis cocks the trigger and raises the gun. Nick confronts him.

"Louis, you can't go on cheating and killing. No, this won't solve your problems."

Alan is watching me, enjoying every second of my agony and indecisiveness. Clearly, it's now or never. I've got to do something. My career is basically over; what have I got to lose? As Nick and Louis talk, leading up to the cold-blooded murder, the stage manager leads me around to the stage door entrance to the office. Then, on a signal from the director, he cues me to enter. Oh Shit!

I draw a deep breath and launch myself through the flimsy door. Pumped for action, I've got to yell something.

"Run, Nicky, run! Run, Nicky run!"

There's really nothing else to do but throw myself on the Gorilla's gun, heedless of danger and ridiculousness, tumbling to the floor, a fool with complete conviction; that's why I'm on the floor, totally spent. But at least I really felt it. That means a lot when you're acting, makes it more believable somehow.

The gun has catapulted across the room and Nick grabs it, before helping me up from the floor.

"Did I do it? Are you all right, Nick?"

He pulls me fondly to his side. "You were first class. Couldn't have done it better myself. My darling, you were magnificent."

"Cut"

The crew applauds us, and we applaud them. Then Nick, the two now untied commissioners and even Alan applaud my feat of derring-do. My face flushes. I bow and try to gracefully accept the accolade. The crew on a film set is the toughest audience a performer ever faces, but when you do something special, their approval is the sweetest reward. I feel as light as air.

Alan smiles at me. I guess I showed him. But his grin is too big, and his hand clapping is a delicate mockery of applause. He's a very irritating man. But he can't rob me of my triumph.

Nick gives me a gentlemanly kiss on the cheek.

"Hooray for you! And we got it in one perfect take."

Elated, riding high, I walk back with them to the green room. I turn to Alan, very full of myself, and say;

"You see, I can do it. I can be heroic. I can do romance. I saved Nick's life, didn't I?"

Alan's smile grows broader. "Tell her the truth, Nick."

Nick's face falls a little. He blinks a few times in confusion, before regaining his usual poise.

"I'm still grateful and proud of her—even though the gun wasn't loaded; but she didn't know that."

Alan falls into a chair in the green room, smiling his head off. He does a high falsetto version of 'run, Nicky, run', which he seems to find just hilarious.

I'm furious. I've been set up. "Your gun wasn't loaded?" I demand icily of Nick. "So Louis couldn't have shot you...or me?"

A Rogue, A Pirate, and A Dry Martini

Remembering the way Alan needled me to get me to go on, I want to punch the SOB right in his rather large nose. Actually, given said nose's thickened bridge, I'm sure he's been the recipient of just such a tribute before.

"You tricked me. You deliberately made a fool of me."

"Aw come on. Can't you even take a joke?"

"Well, I guess you got your big laugh for today."

Nick lights a cigarette for me. "No, not at all. You did just what you were supposed to do. And you did it beautifully. It was heroic and showed you have great courage. How could you know that I had planned surprise Louis when he wasn't carrying his piece, hoping he'd go for my unloaded gun? I knew he might brag a bit before he did me in—make a complete confession. The police were in the office next door, taping everything."

"Well, I feel like a first class idiot. Why didn't you tell me your plan?"

"We had to act quickly. The police didn't give me the chance. You tried to save my life. You have nothing to feel foolish about."

"You guys made a sucker out of me."

"So a hero is a sucker to you?" Alan says, even more disgusted with me. "I'll remember that next time you need rescuing."

"I'll bet you think you're a real hero, just because you play one in the movies. Well, you're just a show-off. As a matter of fact, I think even a lot of real heroes are on ego trips. Guys trying to look big and important. It's such a load of baloney. Men just love to think of themselves as heroes. Go ahead, Alan, tell me I'm wrong."

"Okay. You're wrong. I think one person can make all the difference, if they have right on their side."

Marcy Casterline

Now he's taking me a little more seriously than before. Perhaps his convictions are a little shaken. It's not quite so simple as he makes it seem. And I'm not letting him off the hook.

"Oh, come on, everyone always thinks they have right on their side," I continue, emboldened.

Alan shrugs. This is too deep for him. He's in over his head in a discussion of philosophy. But Nicky, ever the thinking man, takes over the debate.

"I beg your pardon, but we both know Louis The Gorilla was wrong. He thought it was all right to do anything to get rich, even kill. He was the cause of several innocent people's deaths."

I've got a full head of steam, now, and I'm not letting these guys get away with this kind of nonsense. "Oh, innocent people! What does that mean? The jockeys who took payoffs? Women like Lulu, making a living by blackmail? Hey, if you live like that, what do you expect?"

Nick regards me with bewildered concern.

"Lulu was no saint, I grant you. She got greedy. She strayed off the straight and narrow. She was tempted, and she gave in. But does that mean she deserved to die?"

He asks this all so reasonably, that I'm forced to think a little harder.

"It's sort of her own fault, isn't it?" That doesn't sound right, even to me. "So why *do* you solve these cases? To make a living? To get famous? Why?"

"I have something of a reputation with the police departments of various cities, but I'm hardly famous; and I don't want to be. I simply like making things turn out right."

This is not going as planned. I should be winning this. Searching for a culprit, I fix my gaze on Alan, who throws up his hands like I'm holding a gun on him.

"Don't look at me. Sailors hardly ever get famous."

I sigh with deliberate vehemence, for lack of a good retort.

"I just don't get you guys. You don't act like normal people. I need a break. I'm going outside to have a cigarette. I know I don't have to go outside, but let me tell you, all this smoking inside is going to get you into trouble. And, by the way, where do they hide the bottled water around here?"

Nick, who has surely never in his life wanted water in a bottle or any other vessel, nevertheless, with a vague wave of his hand, replies, "the commissary has the only bottled spring water that I know of. There's bottled Coke in the icebox."

"Right," I acknowledge grimly. I can't even get a bottle of water. I grab a Coke from the truly ancient refrigerator. Boy! Is this production company cheap or what? Without a backward glance at my two antagonists, I trudge out of the green room and across the set, dodging the crew who are busy hefting scenery flats, re-hanging overhead lights, moving prop sofas, tables and lamps on and off the set in the cavernous, dusty, dark stage building.

Reaching the side exit we used for Robin Hood, I push the bar on the heavy exit door and step out onto the sunny back lot, still lush with green potted trees and bushes—Phony Sherwood. I light up. I'm so well trained by the anti-tobacco crowd that it feels much more natural to smoke outside, like an exile and a pariah. In fact, I believe I relish the whole furtive, stolen and illicit pleasure, the rebel-without-a-cause aspect of smoking more than the cigarette itself.

How they're getting away with smoking on this set, I really can't figure out. There's always one anti-smoking fanatic whose sole purpose in life is to make smokers miserable. I'm sure somebody will report it, and by tomorrow, cigarettes on stage will be verboten.

The bottled Coke is a real surprise, too. I'd forgotten how much less carbonation there is in bottles, and consequently, how sweet and syrupy a bottled Coke is. I savor a few sips, while I try to calm down.

But no bottled water. What a cheap set. Bernie really sold me out to a bottom feeding Production Company. Cheap interiors for all these rug shows, not much location work. Scripts, what there are of them, so corny and sappy, they must have cost all of four cents. No wonder no one pays any attention to them. And the director and all the actors are complete unknowns, including Bernie. But it's okay for him. He has a real career as an agent. For me, I'm an actress on the way to being a faded name. How did I sink so low so quickly?

This company should be called Loserville Productions. Movies made by people who can't cope without a drink and a cigarette. But who *can* cope in this lousy business? People like Justin. Oh, he copes just fine. What did I ever see in that guy?

I suppose some allowances have to be made for youth and inexperience. I was a kid when we met, just like Melissa Jones. He was three years older, a very knowing, glib, fast talking producer. But in all fairness, he was intelligent. And his uncle was an agent at William Morris— he was virtually a made guy in Hollywoodland.

A Rogue, A Pirate, and A Dry Martini

He's a slick, convincing, confident guy and, ultimately, insincere. But I always knew that. I thought that was the way people were—out for themselves. His professions of love and admiration were well done. He liked to say those things and show me off around town. I was glad to go along for the ride, and he was glad to have someone to take along—anyone with enough Hollywood heat would do. I knew that if he could have dated a movie star, he'd have dumped me in a hot minute. And the same was true of me. We stayed in our sorry, passionless relationship because neither one of us could do any better—until I got cancelled—enter Melissa Jones.

The good news is I'm not heartbroken. But to be so blatantly and insensitively dumped on my last day at my job proves beyond a shadow of a doubt that Justin wasn't even a real friend to me. I'll have to be more careful in the future. I was certainly very much deceived in him. There was even less there than I ever thought.

I light up another naughty smoke and draw deeply. A half dozen grips, pulling wheeled dollies for moving scenery, troop out the exit beside me. Then they begin loading and carting away the dozens and dozens of potted bushes, assorted shrubbery, and small trees that filled in between the few real trees on the back lot to create the look and feel of a properly bosky English forest.

Phony Sherwood is starting to look distinctly sad. The illusion of a woodland glen is fading fast. They're also disassembling the thatched roof Tudor cottage, which was just a flat front facing the camera. It looked real enough, unless you walked behind it and saw the two by fours holding it up. Even the ivy–vine–like ropes used by Robin and his merry men to swing down from the trees are getting pulled off the large fake oak tree. They were like a Disneyland attraction for kids to climb on and now they're being torn down.

The whole sylvan atmosphere is evaporating before my eyes, which are getting a little misty. Does this remind me of my career? One minute I had it all, thought I had something to offer the world as an actress. Then, snap! It's over, like it never happened.

In a very visceral way, it's terribly sad to lose Phony Sherwood. The set designer must have worked so hard to recreate a Sherwood Forest, a mythical Arden. Dare I say it? It was so...pretty. But 'pretty' is a dirty word these days. It's about the lamest, most insulting adjective you can use about anything or anyone in Hollywood, the most disparaging, nasty remark you can make about an actress. Oh God! Please don't let me be *pretty*! For Heaven's sake, the only way Nicole Kidman or Charlize Theron could get their Academy Awards was by getting unglamorous and downright ugly, and Nicole even had to wear a funny nose. All this so they wouldn't be, God Forbid, *pretty*.

Omygod! That's it, isn't it? That's my fatal flaw as a person and an actress. I'm nothing but a mindless, outré, petty bourgeoisie who's a sucker for 'pretty'. How banal! How mundane! How unintellectual! That's why I'll never make it beyond a dopey TV series and why I've been sent to career Siberia—I'm shallow, and my talent and brain are mediocre, schlocky. And even now, knowing how shameful it is, I must honestly admit that I liked Phony Sherwood. And handsome, daring, noble, mischievous, downright sexy Robin Hood set my heart aglow. I wanted him badly, wanted him in the worst way. Yes, I did. And I loved the chance to be *pretty* Maid Marion, princess for a day, with a tart but sweet-tempered retort for Robin, when needed, and a tiara—absolute bliss.

A Rogue, A Pirate, and A Dry Martini

It's no secret that you have to be more than a good actress to make it in Hollywood, these days. It takes brains, too. Like you have to at least have heard of Kafka and Virginia Woolf, and people like that. No one in Hollywood is expected to actually read them, or read any book. Only boring people with too much time on their hands because no one is casting them in any movies have time to read books.

No, to make it in Hollywood you have to be intellectually gifted and painfully sensitive. The 'pretty', 'the happy ending' is what you have to give the audience if you want your project to be *commercial* (another dirty word). The ugly is what wins awards. Hollywood's true artists crave the blasted hopes, understand and sympathize with the senselessly cruel psychopath, feel the pain of the blatantly unjust punishment, scorn, revile and impute despicable motives to all authority figures of any stripe, but especially a priest or a soldier, zealously defend the incestuous or perverse love affair, and are stuck dumb with admiration of scene after beautifully shot scene of revolting, gruesome violence, sexual degradation, and persecution—this and only this is the stuff of real art.

Sometimes I like that arty stuff. Mostly, I don't. So I guess I really don't have what it takes. They found me out. I'm really just a common, ordinary person, nothing special about my intellect at all. What a day of revelations. The worst wound so far is finding out I'm not as cool as I thought I was. Well, I guess I can stop wearing black, because I'm not fooling anyone.

Perhaps that's why I actually kind of like my co-stars here. They're as hopelessly uncool as I am, but they don't seem to know it. Or maybe they don't care. Whatever. But their blind optimism about what they're doing is very winning. Poor fools. Like any of these guys will ever make a living in show biz—yeah right! There's not a Leonardo DiCaprio or Matt Damon style tortured Adonis among 'em. Even Robin, good looking as he is, lacks the facile perfection of a George Clooney or Brad Pitt. Old Robin is a little rough around the edges, and dammit, I like that about him.

The Sherwood green forest has now almost completely reverted to Burbank brown desert. As I watch the grips and stagehands finish up, I realize that there's something missing, something wrong with the picture, but I can't quite put my finger on it.

When it hits me, an actual icy chill runs down my spine. NO CELL PHONES, NO PAGERS! NO HEADSETS! No ring tones and no one is air talking. How eerie! Have they banned cell phones? I guess it wouldn't be a bad idea, but there's *always* somebody with a headset so the stage manager and director can keep in contact.

Okay, this is officially creeping me out. I take a last drag, stub out the butt, and head back to my dressing room. I dig my cell phone out to check for messages, hoping for a call from Bernie. But there's nothing. The cell phone won't even go on. Double Weird!

Chapter Nine

Neither Iris nor Dorothy is waiting for me. But there's a costume hanging, all freshly pressed, by the vanity with a note from Iris telling me it's for my next scene.

The outfit is another knock out. Well, maybe they spend all their money on costumes, not bottled water. This one is a chic little striped suit, bias cut for maximum cling, with a flared skirt to show off some leg. I've truly never seen such great clothes. Their construction is artlessly flattering and sexy, without being obvious. And there's a cute little hat, so I don't need to do more than run a brush through my hair.

Quickly stripping down to bikinis, I throw on a silk kimono dressing gown to freshen up my make-up. I'm almost done, when there's a knock at the door, and Alan peeks in. with a sheepish grin.

"I just wanted to make sure that you'd come back. We're up next."

"I'm back," I reply, civilly, not really angry with him any longer. I realize now that this is obviously just where I belong, and I'd better get used to it. "I'll be ready in a minute."

My low spirits and sense of weary resignation must show, because he looks even more concerned and steps into my dressing room.

"Are you okay?"

"I'm fine. Really." But a big sigh unintentionally escapes, giving away my real feelings.

Alan comes up behind me, putting his hands gently on my shoulders, as he bends down till we're head to head, facing the mirror, and talking to our reflections.

"I hope I didn't do anything to make you feel bad," he says, with warmth and sincerity. "You really were great in your 'run, Nicky, run' scene. You've been pretty good all day. A real trooper. I was only having a little fun with you."

He's whispering in my ear. His strong hands on my shoulders make me very aware that I'm practically naked under this kimono, naked and longing to be touched and caressed by him. I smile and blush a little. His presence is absolutely electric, like nothing I've ever felt before. He's looking at me with that half-amused, half-hungry look of his. What a turn on. But it's more than that. He's a guy who sends you right back to your default setting—woman, all woman, all female—with a man who is supremely aware and appreciative of womanliness, who ignites all the feminine instincts. Like Iris, I can't seem to develop an immunity to his charms, and I feel absolutely no regret about that. He's right; a sex scene with him would be way beyond an X rating, and on screen, totally unnecessary.

"What are you smiling about," he asks, mock gruffly, kidding around with me. "You're in big trouble, you know."

"Am I?" The mere thought leaves me breathlessly *thrilled.*

He straightens up, and I can't help but notice he's one sexy guy, all dressed up in his Captain's whites. I stand up and face him. He draws a deep breath, and his eyes quickly take in my state of semi-undress from head to toe. Our eyes lock, and it's obvious that he's as eager to kiss me, manhandle me and indulge in lots of heavy breathing, as I am to do the same to him.

"So I guess, on stage, we're about to end our stormy, no pun intended, little affair. The Captain dumps the show

girl." I pout fetchingly. "And you sail off into the sunset
with your oh-so-refined lady love. Boy do I hate movies
with a moral. Why do the fun girls always get punished?"

"You punished? You're too cute to punish. This is a
romance, after all."

"You keep saying that, but I don't think this is
romance. Romance is a pathetic, female fantasy about
being helpless and needing to be rescued by some too,
too gorgeous, wonderful Mr. Perfect. And well, you're
cute and sexy, but not that good looking, and certainly no
Mr. Perfect."

"And you're about as helpless as a revolution. When
you talk about movies, they sound so bland and boring.
Romance is about sex...and adventure...and love."

"I thought you said there were no sex scenes," I say,
moving in on him.

"Did I?" he murmurs, his eyes getting dreamy. He's
breathing hot and hard with desire, and so am I. I raise my
arm to push my hair off my face, always a good come on,
and my kimono slips off one shoulder. With his patented
X-rated smile, he readjusts my kimono back onto my PG
shoulder.

"That's a pretty thin little piece of silk, you've almost
got on."

"It's easy to take off," I suggest helpfully.

"I know you've got it all, baby. But that won't help you
now. Remember the pirates. "(He lifts his bandaged foot)
Well, I'm pretty sure they had friends on the ship, and I
think you know something about it."

"Wait a minute. If this is romance, shouldn't *you* be
rescuing *me* from the pirates? Or is it the other girl you
rescue?"

Instead of answering, he starts issuing me orders, as he heads for the door, just as if he were a real captain.

"Get into your costume. Jamesie, your partner in crime, will be waiting for you on the set. You'd better get going."

I do get going. I insert myself between Alan and the door.

"Sure, toots, I'll get ready." I give him the coyest come hither look I've got, my eyes begging for a kiss, my arms around his shoulders. "Can't we just forget about the scene for a minute?"

"No...we can't." He firmly disengages, but doesn't look happy about it. "You've been a bad girl and gotten us both into trouble."

"But you can't resist me, can you?"

"We'll see about that. Now go on."

He turns me around and sends me back into my dressing room with a firm, but very possessive slap on my fanny.

"Don't get fresh with me, pal."

"Pipe down sister. Someday, we'll have a long debate about who got fresh with who."

He's gone. All I can think for a moment is Wow! I am *so* leaving the studio tonight with that guy. I have to get to know him better. Where's he from? Where's he been hiding? Suddenly, I don't give a hoot that my career is in the dumper, I just have to get to know this guy better, much, much better. And Bernie will be happy, because this guy really is hardly in show biz at all. He's the perfect guy to take with me to Peoria.

Eager to get back to work, I don my chic suit and check myself out one last time in the full-length mirror. I make a final adjustment of my smart little hat, setting it at a more rakish angle and pulling a few curls out around the edges. Gosh! I look terrific, if I do say so myself. Honestly, I didn't know I *could* look this good. Shows you what the right clothes can do for you. And there's nothing like the feeling of walking onto the set looking great. Iris has even laid out a cute matching little handbag and white gloves. I think I'll just carry them, use them as a prop, if I need something to do with my hands.

The green room is deserted, as I cross through it. Nick must be in his dressing room, sleeping off all those martinis. But the stage is full of activity. They're setting up the Captain's cabin with its nicely polished, wood paneled walls, built-in desk, bureau, and sofa. It's all trimmed with polished brass. Very snug and nautical.

Alan is seated at his desk with his bandaged foot up on a stool, center stage.

Jamesie, my friend and nemesis is waiting for me ringside, and he's all dressed up, too.

"Bernie, look at you!"

"Yeah, I'm all ready."

He answers to the name Bernie, and he looks a lot like Bernie, but somehow, I've begun to think he's not my Bernie, maybe a cousin or uncle. But he resembles my pal so much that I feel right at home with him.

"And here you are Dolly. You look wonderful."

"You, too. We're like an old married couple all dressed up for Sunday school."

He laughs. "Jamesie and Dolly in Sunday school? Not a chance. We start the scene on the set next to this one, in my cabin."

We walk past the main set, and Alan glances my way with a smile. The stagehands fuss around him, dressing the set with all sorts of appropriate gear: log books, navigation maps, handheld telescope, a barometer for the wall and a tray with a silver pitcher and some glasses.

Jamesie hustles me to the small, one camera set next door. It's supposed to be his cabin, but it's little more than a cabin door, a porthole, and a cushioned chair.

"They want you to start the scene pacing around; then sit down when I tell you to, okay?"

"Sure." I can't imagine what's coming next, but I guess I get found out to be the cheap tart, the little TV actress without the talent or brains to be the leading lady. Great. Even in a stupid romance picture, I can't cut it.

"Roll camera. Action!"

I pace. It's easy. I am worried about myself. I hope I can pull this next scene off and not look like a complete fool in front of Alan. Guilty scenes are hard to play; I mean you have to actually do some acting. When I get close to Jamesie, who's peeking out the porthole, he puts his hand on my shoulder and forces me into the chair. This is my chance to play with the handbag and gloves, which I do, very nervously.

"Sit down, Dolly. Stay calm. He can't prove a thing. You were very sharp to hide that half a hundred-dollar bill so well. Why, Dolly, I couldn't have done it better myself. Right under his nose in your cigarette cartons in his cabin. Without that bill, he's got no evidence. He searched all the cabins, but he didn't find a thing."

"Yeah, yeah. So why does he want to see us?"

"Just a formality."

There's a knock at the door.

"Well, let's get this over with my little dove. When we get out of this, it's you and me, kid."

"Cut"

A Rogue, A Pirate, and A Dry Martini

We're escorted to the Captain's Cabin by a stagehand and shown where to sit. I'm facing Alan in a chair, and Jamesie is behind me on the built in sofa.

"Action!"

Alan begins, "I've asked you two here for a little informal hearing to ask a few questions, if you don't mind."

"Ask away, Captain," Jamesie replies, with an anxious over-confidence that betrays how worried he is. What an actor! To show so much with so little effort. "We've got nothing to hide. You know me, Alan, I'm not that kind of guy."

"Yeah, I know you." Alan says it without a smile. Then to me, "what about you? Have you got anything you'd like to report? (I shake my head 'no' and try to look innocent, but I can't quite pull it off—hey, Dolly's a bad girl, but not a hardened criminal—so I drop my eyes away from Alan's searching gaze.) "No, huh? Well, somebody stole my key to the ship's arsenal, which sure made it easy for the pirates, and they seemed to know all about the bank deposits we were carrying."

"You mean you *were* carrying the bank deposits?" Jamesie asks with wonderfully overplayed hearty surprise, which only barely hides his frustration and disappointment at being beaten and not getting the gold.

Alan eyes him suspiciously. "That's right. It was hidden, and they didn't find it."

"Well, golly," Jamesie feigns an aw-shucks naiveté. "You sure fooled those pirates. And you didn't even tell when they put the boot on you. Do you mind telling me, Captain, where did you hide that money?"

"It was hidden in the steamroller that was tied up on deck. And the money is safely delivered."

The make-up man steps in while the camera is on Alan, and spritzes Jamesie with beads of sweat. When he's back on camera, he pulls out a handkerchief and pats his forehead.

"That was a terrible thing that happened to you, Alan. Makes me queasy just to think of it. Ah, Dolly, have you got a cigarette?"

He gives me a look. Now's our chance to retrieve the only evidence that can implicate us. My cigarette boxes are in Alan's bureau with the torn bill hidden in one.

"Oh Jamesie, I'm all out. Alan, do you mind if I get my cigarettes out of your drawer?"

"No, no," Alan replies. "Go right ahead. Help yourself."

But when I get to the drawer, there are no cartons...no hidden half hundred-dollar bill. This is it. We're cooked.

"They're not here. I wonder what happened..."

"Is this what you're looking for?" Alan holds up the torn bill.

I'm on my feet. I know exactly how to play this. This is my chance to let him have it.

"You rat. You knew it all the time. Well, I tried to warn you. I came to you cabin, but you threw me out like a cheap tramp! And Jamesie caught me by your door. I had no choice but to throw in with him. That's how he got the key. I guess I'm just not good enough for you."

My chest hurts from holding back the sobs that are aching to burst out. This scene hits a little too close to home. I just don't seem to be good enough for anybody.

Alan stares at me gravely for a long beat.

"This has got to be reported to the authorities. You'll go to jail. I'm sorry."

Jamesie has gotten himself a glass of water. He takes a big swallow and then says:

"Aw, Alan, don't be so hard on her. It's not her fault. I had this heist planned long before she got aboard. She had nothing to do with it."

"Well, I'm afraid you'll both have to take what's coming to you," Alan says with a grim sigh.

"Not me. I've outfoxed you this time, Alan," Jamesie says, suddenly slumping down on the sofa.

Alan hobbles toward the sofa, and I'm right behind him. "What the devil did you do?"

"I took some of those tranquilizers I use to keep my livestock calm on a long sea voyage."

I drop to his side, holding his hand. "Jamesie, why'd you do it?"

He clings to my hand, looking into my eyes, his own full of pain, but he's still smiling fondly at me.

"Oh Dolly, I wanted to think you were my girl, that you loved me. If I'd trusted my instincts and thrown you overboard, I'd be okay now. But Dolly, I couldn't do it. Loving you was the only good thing I ever did, and now it's killed me."

He stiffens, as Alan on his other side, supports him. Jamesie's eyes close, he grimaces in pain, then goes slack.

"Jamesie! Jamesie!" I cry. "Try to hang on. We'll get help."

Alan feels his pulse. "It's too late." Alan's face is full of more sadness and compassion than I thought he was capable of. "One of those pills keeps a pig quiet for a whole voyage, and he took a handful. Poor guy, I guess he couldn't stand the idea of jail."

Alan gently pulls me away. "There's nothing we can do for him now."

"I've made a mess of everything." I wipe away the tears. Jamesie's dead. I didn't expect the scene to end this way.

"You couldn't have helped him. Now go to your cabin until we dock. I'll have to hand you over to the authorities."

"Yeah, okay. " I exit with my head hanging and tears flowing.

"Cut"

There's a pause and silence as the crew, stagehands, make-up and hair people also wipe their eyes. Then ecstatic applause breaks out for Jamesie. Why audiences adore you for making them cry like babies is a mystery to me, but they do. All kinds of actors can pump out oceans of salty tears, but it's much harder to make the audience cry. If you can do it, though, you'll have them eating out of the palm of your hand. And boy, Jamesie really pulled the heartstrings in that scene.

Jamesie rises slowly from the couch and bows majestically. Then to the director and all of us;

"Thank you, thank you! How'd I do? I could have taken longer. You know, had a spasm or something but I thought it was more poignant to underplay it."

"You were great, show stopping, scene stealing spectacular!" we all assure him. "Not a dry eye in the house."

"Thank you, see you later. I've got a big change of costume," he says blowing kisses and heading off into the dressing rooms.

The director announces the actors have a half hour break, while they change the set. Alan and I head more or less together back to the green room. No one is around. And except for the hammering and banging of the crew striking the set, it's quiet. The wall clock says three, and I have a pretty good idea how I'd like to spend the next half hour—Alan and I should pick up where we left off. So when he parks himself on a chair and starts unwrapping his bandaged leg, I get us glasses of ice tea and hang around.

"So poor little Dolly goes to jail. Just a cute little chippie, not a lot of brains, but spunky with a good heart. And I must say she dresses well." No response. "So what about you and me? Is that going anywhere?"

Alan raises his eyes from his almost unbandaged leg, scowls, and goes back to his foot.

"Just asking," I say, by way of apology. "Are you someone else's property? Married? Divorced?" I wait, but he says nothing. "Wait a minute, are you saving yourself for your leading lady? She must be a humdinger! I'll bet that's how you got cast in this picture. You're keeping her happy, right?"

Throwing the last of the long ropes of gauze into the trash, he leans back, lights up and just stares at me.

"I guess she has more to offer than I do. Who is she? I'll bet she's some producer's wife, and this is her pet project. They let her finally do this just to shut her up. Am I close?" Nothing. "Well, anyway, I guess she's the one who wins the heart of the brave, but short-tempered Captain. I've got that right, don't I?"

"You think?" he finally responds, nonchalantly. All my attempts to irritate him for the last few minutes have been ignored, barely noticed.

"You're jealous," he says with a slow grin, which for some reason is maddeningly sexy. "I like that in a woman. It means you're in love."

"Not on your life, buster. I just wish I had a better part in this stupid little film, okay?"

"What better part is there than being 'the girl' in a love story?"

"Being 'the girl' is boring and dumb."

"You seem to be having fun doing it. And you're good at it. Hard to find good romantic leads."

"Fun. Okay, you've got me there. I am having fun. But fun doesn't get you anywhere in life. Fun isn't serious."

"I guess that depends on where you want to get in life."

He stubs his cigarette out. He could try to kiss me, if he wanted to.

"So what happens next?" I'm giving him every chance to plant one on my lips.

"You'll see."

He stands up with magnificent unconcern, and walks toward the far end of the green room, where his dressing room is. Just before he opens the door, he turns to me and says:

"Oh, by the way, I'm not married. The other woman got that part because her husband is an agent. And I'm here because I'm under contract to MGM and they loaned me out. See you later."

Chapter Ten

He's gone, again. There's nothing for me to do but retreat into my dressing room, relax on my glorious chaise lounge and have a cigarette, using the very handy and extremely retro stylish, freestanding ashtray. What a luxury to relax in my own dressing room with a cigarette. I could get used to this—in fact, I am getting used to this.

How did I get into it with Alan? I wanted a date with him, and I totally blew it. It's my ego, I guess. Bad girl parts are just as good or even more rewarding to play than the leading lady; but, well, I wanted to be the leading lady. I wanted to win the hero, which I guess is the point of all romances. So I guess I was jealous of whoever is the leading lady. But in love with Alan? We just met, for Pete's sake. It has been fun. But so what? Fun is so nowhere. So trivial. But it's true that I have had fun today, and I guess it shows. The day has flown by, not like work at all, though I've worked harder here than I ever have. Even Morgan Sidney was never as exciting or involving as this. What was it Alan said? Something about being under contact to MGM? MGM doesn't even exist anymore. Was he kidding?

As I think back over the whole day, it all seems kind of strange. Really, how could Bernie have set this up? Maybe he heard about it from his cousin Bernie the actor. But how could they know I'd come into this dressing room? Or that they'd hook up with me just because I was in this building.

I should call Bernie. I try my cell phone, but it doesn't get a signal in here. Going outside is the only solution. It has to be done, much as I'd like a little catnap on the chaise lounge.

Still in costume—and why change when I look so good—I grab my own handbag and head for my dressing room door, the one I entered this morning so full of curiosity about the old studio days. Little did I suspect what was going on here. It's kind of weird that they seemed to be expecting me. Of course, they know who I am from my TV show. I'm sure there's a perfectly rational explanation for everything. But I've got to get some names and addresses and a contract. Well, as soon as I get Bernie on the line, I'll get some answers and work out the details.

The long corridor, which this morning seemed so full of old Hollywood ghosts, is as quiet and dim as ever. Proceeding toward the glass double door exit to the lot, I pass the dressing room where my Morgan Sidney wardrobe is waiting for me, as indicated by a note from my costume mistress stuck on the door. So I am in the right building after all.

Outside, leaning on the stair railing, two steps up from Daffy Duck Drive, I try my cell and get a signal. Just then, I hear someone calling my name; it's Bernie, way down the road, tooling toward me in a fringe topped golf cart. He's waving frantically at me, and I wave back.

The cart jerks to a stop. It lacks the engineering prowess Bernie is accustomed to in his fancy Mercedes. He eases out of the cute, but scarcely comfortable little padded seat, saying;

"I've been trying to get you on the phone for an hour."

"My cell doesn't work inside the building."

"I figured. They're old, too much steel. Built to last forever. Anyway, I finally came looking for you. I've got a meeting for you this afternoon. Very important. It's with Hadley Finch-Scott."

"Hadley Finch-Scott! Wow! Incredible!" I exclaim, forgetting everything else for the moment. "What's it for?"

Finch-Scott is only the hottest Brit Shit director in the world. An English director, which is to say an object of intense veneration in Hollywood, where the concept of aristocracy is so deeply ingrained and practiced with such fervid devotion, it's hard to believe LaLa land is part of America. A British accent of any kind, even Australian, guarantees that the bearer is taken *very* seriously and accorded the status of cultured, refined, highly gifted theatrical demi-god. All are assumed to be direct descendants of William Shakespeare. The only better thing is to be a Swedish, tall, blonde, socialist who believes in free love—the Hollywood wet dream, like Uma Thurman, who has the added attraction of a Buddhist monk for a father. But Finch-Scott really is Mr. Academy Award. And his pictures are big money makers, too. It doesn't get any better.

"It's for a part in his next picture," Bernie explains. "A girl buddy picture. He's doing preliminary meetings with all the big name actresses, but he's looking for a new face."

A new face. I've heard that before, and they never mean it. They always end up with someone who's been acting in Hollywood since they were three—like me, for instance.

"A girl buddy picture," I repeat, my heart sinking. After working with Nick, where we were so much more than buddies, the whole concept seems lacking in so many ways, especially the no kissing ways. But this is a *girl* buddy picture, (I hope I'm not expected to kiss another girl!) and Hadley Finch-Scott is directing. "So what's the story?"

"Two girls at a honky-tonk bar in the sticks meet and hit it off. One girl is raped by an off-duty cop, who she shoots and kills with his own gun. Knowing she'll never get a fair trial in this redneck town, they decide to run for it. Drive cross country. One long car chase. Oh, they shoot more cops, pick up hitchhikers, and blow up trucks. It's terrific! Here's the breakdown for you to look over before your meeting. The appointment is for this afternoon at six-thirty. Great, huh? Maybe your career isn't over. They were thrilled to find out you're free and are dying to meet with you."

'Thrilled and dying' are agent lingo for it didn't take more than fifteen minutes to talk them into taking the meeting.

"They drive cross country and shoot and blow up things. I guess it's better than the usual chick flick where all they do is complain about men and compare their favorite places to shop and shades of lipstick. I guess it's a step in the right direction."

"Yeah, yeah," Bernie agrees enthusiastically.

"Have they signed the male co-star yet?"

"No, no, these women don't need men. It's really exciting stuff. Lots of action. The good stuff that producers love, that only men usually get to do. Gun play, sex, fighting. It'll do great business at the box office."

"Um hum. Nothing like an action flick. Men love to watch other men save the world from disaster, aliens and bad guys. I guess it will be a lot more interesting than one of those women's weepies. Rape, car chases, guns, explosions, danger, excitement." I stifle a yawn. The only thing I find more boring than self-absorbed women's pictures are the relentless, endless car chases and fight scenes so dear to men's hearts. My eyes glaze over, and I get brain freeze.

"Wow! Yeah!" It comes out flat. I try again. Once more with feeling. "WOW! YEAH!"

My acting must stink because Bernie looks worried.

"What's the matter? It's a great idea. An action pix with girls doing the action. You don't seem excited."

"I guess...I'm not. So this is what it's come to—girls have to be like men to find an audience?"

"Hey, it'll be a blockbuster. You'll get all kinds of offers to do anything you want, if you get this."

"Well," I laugh. "I've done some pretty great stuff today, already. I've wrestled Louis the Gorilla, been on a ship in a typhoon, I've even risked my life and my crown to save Robin Hood. All much more interesting than having a car chase with a girl buddy."

"Whaaat? What are you talking about?"

"Don't you know? They said you got me this job. I'll admit I wasn't thrilled at first. They're sort of cheap romances, but these movies have a certain appeal that I can't fully explain."

"What movies? I don't remember signing you on to any project. Are you okay?"

"Bernie...come on, 'fess up. You made a deal for me for these low budget, PG romances. They're shooting them right here on this stage. You tricked me into coming here, but it's okay, even though all the other actors are complete unknowns, I forgive you. But I'm working with a relative of yours. He's got the same name as you, and looks just like you. Is he a distant cousin or something?"

Bernie's frown deepens into creases of total bewilderment. "If you say so. But I don't think they use this stage at all anymore. Haven't for years. I do have quite a few cousins out here, some working in the biz in various capacities. Maybe one's an actor. Bernie is a family name. Back in the Thirties, I had an Uncle Bernie who did pretty well as a character actor. Started out in silent films. Did even better when sound came in."

I stub my cigarette out indignantly. "Well, for Pete's sake, I'm not making this up. I've been working my butt off all morning. In fact, this is one of my costumes. Isn't it great? I'd love to take it home with me."

"Sure, take it. Nobody will ever miss it. Just a lot of old junk down here. But, you know," he says, eyeing me closely, "you do look great. I've never seen you looking so good. Is that a Morgan Sidney costume? She dressed better than I thought."

"Are you kidding? Morgan never dressed this good. But about this job..."

"Yeah, sure. Have them send a copy of the contract to my office, and I'll look it over. Now, I've got to hurry. I was going to take you out to a late lunch. We can grab a bite before your appointment. And I want you to meet a new client I've just signed. I want you two to be friends."

"Really? Who is she? Have I heard of her?"

"Now don't get all upset—it's Melissa Jones. She's just starting out. No competition for you at all. I think you two can help each other."

"Yeah, great," I say, as deadly furious as it's possible to be at Bernie.

"Come on, you're on to better things. This Finch-Scott picture would be a great break for you. They're looking for an independent, intelligent actress. I think it's a new trend. So go change. I'll meet you back at my office, okay?"

"Bernie, I can't. I really can't. Not today. I'm busy here. I've already shot several scenes. They expect me back."

Bernie squints into the building. "Boy, they must be very secretive about what they're doing here. I haven't heard a word about it. Maybe that's why they're shooting on this old stage."

"You must have submitted me and forgotten about it."

"Yeah, yeah, sure. Well, if you're happy, I'm happy. But you're going to do the Finch Scott appointment, right? It's not till six-thirty."

I sigh. "Yeah, I'll be there. Thanks a lot Bernie."

We cheek kiss good-bye. He climbs back into his golf cart. "Later, babe."

He waves, I wave. The tiny battery engine buzzes to life.

"Yeah, Bernie, later...much later," I mumble as the endearingly silly cart joggles away.

A girl buddy picture—car chases, lots of action. Whatever happened to the magic of the movies? Thrill ride movies don't make you feel good, they beat you into submission. I'll meet Finch-Scott to keep Bernie happy, but old Hadley is probably seeing every actress in Hollywood, and who cares?

I take a last contemplative puff on my cigarette, thinking it's odd Bernie didn't know anything about these romance pictures I'm doing, especially since they certainly seemed to be expecting me. I think I may have been right when I thought they were doing some sort of gag reality show, like make your own black and white movie the old fashioned way. And, unbeknownst to Bernie, they set it up so I would be in the area, and they could snag me into working with these unknown actors.

Makes sense, because these guys are not like most Hollywood actors. They aren't stuck up, or stuck on themselves. They really seem interested in the acting. I'll bet they recruited them from small theater companies across the country. Maybe this is sort of an American Idol does American Actor. And they end up finding better, more talented people than the professionals who are already working in the industry. That's got to be the answer. And that's why Bernie hasn't heard about it; it's top secret, until they've got a few shows in the can. Otherwise, actors like me would know instantly what was going on and try to prepare. I guess their plan is to use one real professional for an added gag. Well, I'm game, and it's been fun. Hey, being on American Idol didn't hurt anybody's career.

Back in my dressing room, there's another medieval costume and a note from Iris. I shuck off my favorite chic little suit and hang it up carefully, in case—I hope, I hope—I get to wear it again. Then it's time to go Medieval Marion. This is a new dress, and very attractive one, a clinging, heavy jersey in silver, with long flowing, graceful sleeves and royal blue velvet trim.

This next Robin scene can't be in phony Sherwood, because it's gone. I wonder what I'm up to now, in Merrie Olde England.

Securing the scarf onto my head with a gold braid circlet, I gather my long skirt grandly in hand and enter the green room, fully expecting my co-stars to execute elegant and deep bows as I pass. But no one is there, and the lights are out. Boy, they really take their half hour break seriously around here.

It's not completely dark. One bare bulb service light gets me to the stage door. I plunge through to the stage, all business, ready to go on, but the dusty silence that greets me practically knocks me over. What the heck is going on now? Where is everybody? It's mostly dark here, too. Just like this morning, it's all huge, dark shadows. From high up, few grimy windows cast a grayish twilight over everything. The air has that slightly stale and mildewy odor again. I can't even smell any cigarette smoke. I don't get it.

A little frisson of totally spooked feeling makes my stomach do a flip-flop. Where is everyone? It's been more than a half an hour, they should be back.

Thinking they might be outside in some new phony England scene, I march confidently to the exit and shove the big bar, but it's locked. Hummm. Panic time. Prim Lady Marion turns suddenly, with no regal dignity at all, grabs up her skirts and trots quickly back toward the green room.

"Alan! Alan! Nick! Anybody here?"

No answer. I try all the doors, but the place is deserted. With an increasing sense of panic and urgency, I race back on to the stage. Something is terribly wrong. I try to calm down. This is definitely the stage I've been working on all morning. No mistake about that. But no set is ready for use.

"Okay, you guys," I call out bravely, feeling like a complete idiot and shattering the total silence. "This is a joke, right? You can come out now. You've had your little laugh. Put the lights on. Alan! Nick! Robin! Yoo Hoo! Hello!"

I pause, listening for a snicker, a footfall, any sound that would betray someone's presence. But it's just the creepy buzz of silence. Exploring further, I find some of the props from this morning's work piled against a scene

skein from my Art Deco apartment, and they look as if
they haven't been used in decades. Goosebumps raise the
hair on my arms. "I'm here," I call out hopefully, but
there's only stillness.

None of this fits in with my American Idol theory. If it
was a joke, they'd have come out by now and gotten the
laugh. Making my way carefully though the debris in the
semi-darkness, I head deeper into the vast looming
shadows, with a strange sense of disbelief. This can't be
happening. I start talking to myself to keep from getting
the creeps.

"Hey you guys, where are you? It's me, the gal who
saved you from Louis the Gorilla. You'll need me for the
sequel. Hey Robin! We've got to get Richard back on the
throne. You'll need your Maid Marion, and here I am.
Alan, oh Alan, I know Dolly goofed up, but without me,
you couldn't win the good girl. Where is everybody? Ollie
ollie in free! You win, you can come out now, I give up."

In the dimness, I wander aimlessly around old props,
through set doors on old scenery flats, looking, looking in
vain.

There's no one here. I'm just a silly, nostalgic actress
who got herself all dressed up for nothing. I plop down on
an creaky old three legged stool about eight inches off
the ground. Not very regal. Beautifully clad Maid Marion
gives up.

I've heard of people stumbling into places where
echoes of the past could vaguely be seen. It was
Gettysburg, I think, a place where so much that was tragic
and dramatic happened. Well, I'm sure a lot happened in
this studio. Not on the level of Gettysburg, of course. But
still these stages are old, too and so many dramas,
personal and professional, must have taken place here.

But it didn't feel like that earlier today. If they were all phantoms, they were more real than most of the actors I've worked with. And I want them back. They were so much more fun and daring. Just being with them made me feel alive in a lot of interesting new ways. As if who I was mattered, and who they were mattered and like that was all that was really important.

"What the heck is going on here? Guys, you can't act like none of this happened. It happened. And you know you won't get anyone better than me. Trust me, all the actresses around today are driven, ambitious, neurotic, fanatics or sluts. Come on you guys, I was better than that. You showed me who I was, who I could be...There's nobody here, is there? I'm talking to myself. Dang! It all seemed so real. Shit! I didn't even get to find out how the stories ended."

The lack of response shuts me up. I listen in vain for some sound, some voice in the distance, some hammering, or some laughter to show me there's somebody out there, somebody around somewhere, but there's nothing.

I sigh about fifty times, while I play with my silver gown. But, oh well, what difference does it make? What difference did any of it make? On that happy note, I force myself to stand up and head back to the dressing room. As I retrace my steps, I try to open the last door I came through, but it won't budge. Oh Great.

Half-heartedly and then furiously, I try the stupid door again. But it's stuck tight. A prop malfunction. Good thing they're not filming. How silly I'd look, noble Lady Marion rattling the door handle. It's definitely jammed shut.

I look around and realize that I'm boxed in. Three sides of a dingy gray stone set, all nailed together and pushed up against the studio wall. How did I get myself into this mess? I try the door again. I shake it, pull it, pound it. I use two hands, hurl myself against it, all to no effect.

These sets are all jerry-rigged to last a day or a week at most, just flimsy stuff, easy up and easy down. I should have no problem. Right. But pratfalls, stuck doors, and falling scenery are always the most entertaining part of the gag reels at wrap parties every year. And this one would have everyone on the floor laughing their heads off. But it's not so funny when you're all alone.

I spend another fifteen minutes attacking the door, and pounding and kicking the plywood scenery flats. They shudder under my determined assault, but don't give way. I yell 'help' quite loudly several times. It's a reflex and makes me feel better. But there's no one on this stage, and it's a soundproof stage. No one outside can hear anything.

Thoroughly spent, I retreat back to my stool. Apparently I'm stuck here till somebody finds me. Thank God Bernie knows that I'm here. Otherwise, I'm so far off the beaten path, I might not be found for years. I can see it all now, a mysterious skeleton turns up on an old, unused stage—could it be that TV actress who disappeared so many years ago? Oh goody, I've scared myself to death.

But there are worse things than being scared, like losing hope that I have a future as an actress; like losing the chance to finally do some good work; like losing three really fun guys, who have become my standard of what a man should be, if at all possible—smart, good-looking, game, not too serious, unaffected, but competent, and most important—martini drinkers and great kissers. I'm so sick of muscle bound Rambos and pretty boy action heroes. I've had more than enough of the masculine vanity parade.

Damn, this is getting scary. I could be trapped in here for hours. Not that I'm missing anything. I could have been trapped in here for the last five years and not missed much. Just Morgan Sidney, child of the used-to-be-small screen that's not so small anymore—it's the men and women in the production offices who got small. Men and women producers who are old enough to know better, or know something, but don't, and don't want to; who only want their big paychecks to keep arriving in their mailboxes and will do literally anything (except think and be creative) to keep them coming. I think that sums up television today: the last resting place of the terminally untalented.

In spite of all those morons, I'm proud of Morgan Sidney. I fought for her soul—that crazy, laughing twenty-something, single, independent, private eye with a nosey streak a mile wide, just a Mid Western gal whose weapon of choice was common sense with a chaser of pungent wit. We were good, and that's dangerous in TV land. They don't want discerning viewers. It's a monopoly franchise ordained by the FTC. Why screw it up by startling the audience out of their TV torpor with something original? If they want something good, they can damn well rent it, buy it, or use pay TV. Otherwise, we don't rock the boat; just keep the money machine purring along.

But I was a dreamer; aren't we all when we start out? Just an dumb, idealistic kid who didn't know any better and wanted to make good. Theater people are dreamers, "such stuff as dreams are made of", and storytellers, an old profession, even older than that famous "oldest profession", if you want my opinion. And sitting here on this stool, trapped on a stage set, wondering where my fellow players are, I'm at a kind of reality intersection, one of those places where dreams and reality meet. They often do, in Hollywood. We all know the stories of Cinderella stars, monster stage mothers, Prince Charmings who turn out to be frogs.

My favorite Hollywood meets fairy tale intersection is the famous actress who decided that all apples were poisoned with pesticide, refused to eat them and went on TV and urged other people to stop eating the poisoned apples. What could be more Snow White Freudian than refusing to eat the apple of desire, especially if your stock and trade as an actress is being a frigid, blonde ice maiden? The actress was of course, Meryl Streep and her Alar scare. Talk about your acting out your neurosis in public. But let's face it, if it had been Meryl in the Garden of Eden, instead of Eve, none of us would be here. She certainly wouldn't have tasted the apple; all she'd worry about was if the snake was an endangered species. I mean can you picture Meryl committing an original sin? I can't even picture her committing an unoriginal sin. Thank God.

So why am I the second tier actress and she's the untouchable star? Go figure.

But I liked my work this morning. I was in it up to my neck playing a person coping with life's problems. Like Alan said, it's kind of a metaphor. I confess, being 'the girl' was great! It's really all I ever wanted to be—the girl who goes out and tries and fails miserably, but figures out how to pick herself up and accomplishes something, or falls in love with the wrong guy, who seems like the right guy, but isn't, or falls in love and screws it up, but after a struggle, lives happily ever after.

I want to believe in the happy ending with the girl and guy getting together. I really do. I want to overcome my cynical side, the sneering scorner, the rotten waster in me who expects the Vlad the Impalers, and is surprised and baffled by the Louis Pasteurs. I want to believe. Hell, that's why I became an actress and stayed an actress, I can't help believing in believing. I yearn for that feeling of believing, that sense of trying to shoot for an ideal. I used to think it was some kind of elemental life force. You know, the reason why chimps walked out onto the savannah and started talking to each other. But that's not enough to explain Mozart, I'm afraid, or even Daffy Duck. Better minds than mine have tried to explain and only ended up looking colossally stupid, so I won't try. It's there, that need to believe. I've caught it like a flu bug you can't shake that keeps your muscles aching and gives you a fever; it comes and goes like malaria, but it's always there.

And like malaria, I'm feverishly yearning again for Alan, for his kiss and to have his arms around me. And for Nick's kiss, which was wonderful, breathtaking, and suggestive of sophisticated fun, dancing all night in tuxedoes and daring evening gowns. And for Robin's kiss, and to be in his arms for a night; all that boisterous, manliness, all his fiery spirit at your command; that would be something. He is a man among men, no doubt. But, the man I want is Alan. He's not the man I want to want. I'm sure the other two would be much easier to handle, but he's it for me.

And it was all real. Very real. Every kiss, every heated glance was real. It must have been. I couldn't have dreamed it all up. But if I didn't dream it all up, where did they all come from, and where did they go?

Jeeze, I wish I had a cigarette. Why didn't I think to bring my smokes with me? In desperation, I prowl my dark, little prison again, sure that I saw an ashtray somewhere. There it is, an elegant metal ashtray stand with a large glass bowl, and a center compartment loaded with cigarettes and matches. I can't believe it. This is too weird. No sound stage in America has cigarettes on it, anymore, and these are...My God! Filterless Chesterfields! And they're American made. Where the heck did they find them? Where the Heck am I? Nineteen thirty-five, for Pete's Sake? But oh, lighting one up is just heaven. Just knock-your-socks-off smooth tobacco high.

I have no answers, and, furthermore, with all the cigarettes I could possibly need to see me through my little crisis, I don't care. I'm happy just smoking and remembering the scenes I did, feeling proud and excited. If I ever get out of here—let's be optimistic, when I get out of here—no one will ever believe this. Heck, I hardly believe it myself, except for these divine Chesterfields— now that's pretty hard to explain away, except if I smoke them all before I get rescued.

Suddenly, I hear the clash of swords and voices.

"Don't be a fool, Robin. You'll never take the castle. You don't have enough men. I have a thousand soldiers at my beck and call."

I jump dizzily to my feet. Filterless Chesterfields really pack a punch. I can't believe it! They're back! It is Prince John! He's mocking Robin, as the swords ring steely death. I stub out the ciggie, hide the ashtray, and

run breathlessly to the door, waiting for my cue. Then
Robin boldly, even laughingly, replies:

"But I wonder whose side they'll fight on when they
find out King Richard is with us!"

"King Richard? So he *is* back." Old Prince John does
not sound happy to see his brother.

"Yes, no thanks to you. He is here to claim his rightful
throne. What have you done with Maid Marion?"

My heart beats frantically. However it happened,
whatever is going on here, it's not over. Thrills of joy
transport me. Robin, even fighting for his life, is thinking
of his Maid Marion. He's a wild, free man, probably
impossible, but devoted to me.

Prince John answers:

"She was tried for treason, and she's to be burned at
the stake, even as we speak. Last I saw her, she was
locked in the dungeon, but you'll never get to her in time.
I'll see to that. Men, seize this villain! Obey, you curs! I
order you! What's the matter? Wait, where are you going?
Here you are at last. You're the Sheriff of Nottingham,
make them obey!"

"Prince John..."

"Prince John? I'm King John!"

"Your highness, your brother has returned. He is the
King. I think we'd better get out of here, before he has us
arrested."

"Too late," Robin cries. "Arrest these men and take
them away. Halt a moment, Sheriff, and hand over the
keys to the dungeon. I must free Maid Marion."

I hear keys jingling. Robin flings the door open. This
is my cue and his moment. I stumble weakly out the door
and fall into Robin's waiting arms.

"Robin!"

"Maid Marion," he cries, clasping me to him. "Are you alright? I feared I would be too late, my darling."

He holds me tightly in an embrace. Behind him, I see camera, lights, and stagehands on the set. I found my way to the great hall of the castle and ended up in the dungeon, just where I was supposed to be. Odd, very odd, indeed. But I'll think about that later. Right now, King Richard is entering in full regal robes, and a crown. He's a tall, kingly man, a real Lionheart. Perfect casting. Twenty men in colorful, medieval tunics and carrying swords follow him onto the stage. With a smile, he addresses Robin.

"Robin, I see you've taken care of Prince John, as well as Lady Marion. Come, Sir Robin of Locksley, you have restored the throne of England to its rightful heir. I am forever in your debt. Ask any boon of me, and I shall grant it."

Robin takes my hand as he answers the King.

"Sire, that which I want cannot be granted by Kings or laws. It is the love of the Lady fair. She alone can give me her heart."

Robin falls to his knees at my feet. My face flushes in pleasure and embarrassment. I've never had a man kneel to me. My chest swells in pride, and my heart is bursting in gratitude. He's rescued me, he loves me, and he has made my dreams come true. I feel a little faint.

"My Lady, I know you to be the most beautiful, brave, and gracious of all the ladies in the land. I have pitifully little to offer you: my strong right arm, my honor, and my deepest love. My character and my past exploits are well known, and I cannot hide from you that life with me may be fraught with danger and adventure. Lady, I would risk any danger for one kiss from those fair lips. Say you will be mine and make me the happiest of men."

I look into his pale blue eyes, so handsome, so full of ardent passion, and I speak my heart. With a gracious smile, I extend my hand to him, beckoning him to rise to his feet.

"Robin, when I was alone and forgotten in the dungeon, it seemed as if there was no past or future, only death. You saved me from that cruel fate. Yes, Robin, I shall marry you."

He rises and embraces me. "We shall live in the Greenwood forever."

Bells peal, pandemonium breaks loose in the great hall among the soldiers and the Merry Men of Sherwood who now enter. They are cheering Robin and their rightful king, raising their swords and throwing garlands. Robin takes my hand, and smiling happily, we slip offstage.

"Cut!"

The director ends the scene, and Robin keeps my hand in his, but I don't care. All I know is that everyone is back. The stage is alive with extras, stagehands, script girls, and costume and hair people. It's all here, and all very real. I pinch myself, and it hurts, just like it should. Whatever is going on, I'm enjoying myself too much now to think about it. I'm happier than any mere mortal deserves to be, and I know how lucky I am. Robin has pulled me into his arms, though clearly the scene is over.

"You were wonderful. You always are. I bluster and fight, but you're my true heroine."

He kisses me gently on the lips, I'm so surprised and pleased that I let him.

"That's for you, for being such a splendid actress," he says, still unwilling to let go of me.

"Thank you," I reply shyly, knowing my good fortune, for once. "That's the very nicest of compliments."

He leads me toward the exit door.

"Where are you taking me?"

"To my trailer for a drink."

Of course, in real life, he's obviously a full-fledged skirt chaser.

Fortunately at that moment Iris appears from the stage with an armful of medieval armor.

"Come on you two, Get out of those clothes so I can send them to be cleaned."

I say good-bye and follow her meekly through the green room, where I see Alan in his whites and Nick in a tweedy sports jacket. We greet each other with friendly hellos as I pass through on my way to my dressing room, and it all seems perfectly normal, too normal to ask any silly questions about.

Chapter Eleven

"We're almost done for today, honey. I'll bet you're getting tired," Iris says sympathetically.

"No, not a bit. I hate for it all to end."

"Well, we'll be back tomorrow."

My heart skips a beat. "Yeah, I guess so."

I quickly and efficiently get out of my medieval costume, pat my slightly damp self with the grapefruit size, ostrich feather powder puff, full of scented talcum powder, and spritz myself with an intriguing cologne called Antelope. Then, feeling delightfully refreshed, I'm ready for my next costume, a tweedy suit, like Nick's. I also have a casual felt hat with a long pheasant feather. Very chic me!

"You're all ready for your country drive" Iris says, looking me over carefully, pulling and tugging things, until I meet with her satisfaction.

"Country drive? How do they manage that on an indoor stage?"

"Rear projection. They filmed the road way up at Lake Arrowhead a week ago. When you're done, come back to put on that cute striped suit again. I'll have it ready for you."

Nick is waiting for me, sipping the last of a martini, which he offers me. I take a swallow, and we head out to the set. Just as Iris said, it's all ready for a rear projector shot. There's an old roadster convertible on rockers in front of a large screen with a projector ready to play the film of the passing roadside behind us.

Nick and I get into the car, with the camera in front of us.

"Roll film! Roll projector! Roll camera! Action!"

Nick grasps the wheel and pretends to steer. The rocker panels move us gently, simulating a real road, and a wind machine ruffles our hair lightly, under our fashionable, outdoorsy hats.

"We're dinning out tonight, dear."

"Oh, Nicky, you didn't have to..."

He reaches into the back seat, raises a large picnic basket and hands it to me.

"I didn't."

"A picnic?" I comment, unfolding the gingham cloth to look inside.

"I had it catered at the Plaza. It's considered de rigueur at Saratoga."

"We're going to picnic at the races! Oh how wonderful. Will Three Fingers be there, too?

"He will, and he's got some very hot tips for me."

"Oh Nicky, how nice. Cold chicken, wine, apples, and cheese. This will be the best picnic."

The light fades as if it were evening twilight. I put my head on Nicky's shoulder. What a perfect ending, two pals in love driving off into the sunset. Not as thrilling as bells pealing, and a King's majesty, but very satisfying, in its own way. I sigh happily. Another great ending. What luxury! Only one more to go.

As we walk slowly back to the green room, Nick says:

"Well, I'm sure we'll see each other around. Hollywood is such a small town, you can't help running into everyone you know on the boulevard." He gives me a peck on the cheek.

"The boulevard? Hollywood Boulevard?" I exclaim in surprise. No actor or actress in their right mind goes anywhere near Hollywood Boulevard. Not these days, anyway.

"Naturally Hollywood Boulevard. The best martinis are at Musso and Frank's."

"Oh, Musso and Frank's. Yeah, of course. They're great." For a minute there, he had me going.   Jeeze, Musso and Frank's *is* still on Hollywood Boulevard, but I think they've been there like forever, since the nineteen-twenties, at least.

Nick is the most unflappable, sophisticated man I've ever met. All charm, all grace and that gently sardonic humor and intelligence. I'd rather work with him than any other actors I know, except Alan, and Robin and of course, Jamesie. I'm glad they all came back. I was starting to worry that I'd only dreamed all this.

I wander back to my dressing room, and find Iris has left me my next costume. It's my favorite bias cut suit with hat, bag, and gloves, again. I have one more scene as Dolly, my favorite bad girl. Then I'll decide whether to go to my meeting with Finch-Scott, or try for a little after work fun with Alan.

Dressed again in my favorite striped suit, I'm back on the set, sitting in the captain's cabin with Alan, who is smoking his pipe and has his foot once again bandaged up, although not as heavily as before. And this time, he has a cane to help him walk.

"Action"

"Well, this is it, I guess," I say dramatically, resigned to my fate. Dolly didn't make good, but she's still a spunky trooper, not one to feel sorry for herself. "Send in the Gendarmes. I'm ready."

Alan looks thoughtful and gestures with his pipe to the chair opposite his. "Relax, we've got some time yet."

I sit, waiting for this less than happy ending, less than happy for Dolly, that is. But if I keep my spirits up, I'll win some sympathy from the audience.

"You're awfully quiet, for a change."

I shrug.

He spends some time lighting his pipe while I fiddle with my gloves. Alan is a tough guy, but fair, the last guy in the world you want to cross. I hope I can pull this scene off without dissolving into tears or something equally obvious and clichéd.

"Listen, I've been thinking about what you did."

I straighten up in my chair. "What I did," I say, sighing remorsefully. "The truth is I was angry and wanted to show you a thing or two. You thought you were too good for me. Well, I did try to warn you that night in your cabin, and Jamesie caught me. I *had* to steal that key. But I was wrong. (Tears leak down my cheeks and another big sigh escapes.) And I'm very sorry."

He sighs, looks down, abashed, then at me again, and to my surprise, his eyes are full of warmth and... tenderness. "I've been thinking. What I did was wrong, too. You tried to help, and I didn't listen. Instead, I insulted you, and I did it because I was drunk. I was drunk while on duty, and the Captain's not supposed to do that."

"Aw, you were tired. Fighting that typhoon was hell. But you kept a lot of those people in steerage from being washed overboard, and you saved the ship."

He puts the pipe down, takes my hands in his and looks me straight in the eye. "Dolly, I've decided to turn in my Captain's hat and stay here till your trial. I want the judge to know the whole story. I think when I tell him what you tried to do, that you tried to warn me, I think he'll go easy on you."

"But you won't be a Captain anymore," I point out, knowing what a sacrifice he's offering to make in order to save my ass. And not overlooking how delectable he looks in his captain's whites, can't give those up.

"Oh, they may dry dock me for awhile, but it's what I deserve." Then he pauses and looks me straight in the eye. "It'll give me time to see to some of my personal affairs."

"You mean your fiancée? She won't like it."

"She's not my fiancée anymore. I can't marry her... because I'm in love with you."

I pause, holding my breath and wondering how to play this. It might be true. But no, an ending *that* happy doesn't even happen even in the movies.

"You're making a terrible mistake." I say portentously, dropping a big hint that the bad girl doesn't get the guy. Here I am all ready to play the noble, but naughty girlfriend, and I get thrown a curve ball. Can this possibly be in the script?

"Stop telling me what to do," he sputters in irritation. The short tempered, bossy Captain Alan is back, the only man Dolly could love. Then he gives me a look with his baby blues that would melt Krypton. "I'm in love with you, always have been, always will be. Come here, Dolly," he says standing up and pulling me to my feet.

Then he wraps me carefully and deliberately in his arms. I sort of try to stop him, push him away, which only makes us both hotter. Then he's kissing me. Real kissing. Whoa Baby! Okay, I'm just absolute putty in this guy's arms. Think movie clichés for sexual tension—think fireworks, think starry night with a full moon, think Hawaiian drums pounding away, think Wow. The hell with it. Think anything you want, because I've stopped thinking. Not even sure I can still stand up.

He eases up on the kissing, but still holds me in his arms and that's the only thing keeping me on my feet.

"Let me get my cane, and I'll walk you down to the police station."

Hum, I like it. It's another happy ending. Two juicy people wounded by love end up together. And it's the right ending. Of course these two belong together. The audience will feel how right it is. Gee, three happy endings in one day. And wow, it feels kind of good.

That's it. Fade to black, The End.

"Cut"

And with the unmistakable thwap of the slate, it's over. The dock, the ship's cabin, all the sets start to come down. Everyone is preparing to go home, closing and covering the valuable cameras, turning off lights, clearing away props to the prop shop. Tomorrow, we could come back and be in Manhattan or Timbuktu, and it's all in a day's work.

And I'm back to being me, and Alan is back to being whoever he is.

It's controlled chaos on the stage as everyone is in a rush to head home. They open a big side exit door, and the crew pours out.

Alan and I laugh together the whole way back to the green room. I am definitely leaving the studio with him tonight, no matter what! I want more kissing and more of everything he's got.

"I can't believe that's the way our story ends. I guess romance movies aren't as stupid as I thought," I proclaim, not at all reluctantly.

"I don't know what you've got against romance."

"Nothing at all, not anymore. I like romance now. It's deep, and surprisingly outrageous, but actually somehow, very true to life, not phony baloney, like I thought."

"Yeah, yeah, might just catch on," he replies briskly, as he heads into his dressing room and I into mine.

Iris is waiting for me with my final instructions of the day.

"Hang that outfit up, before you leave. But don't worry about it. That's the last time we need to use it. Okay, honey, see you tomorrow."

Iris has taken off her seamstress smock and is in her street clothes; and she's obviously a vintage clothing nut, (and lots of costume people are) because she's dressed in an unusual bottle green wool crepe dress with shoulder pads that falls past the knee, a real nineteen thirties classic that still looks like new.

After she leaves, I open the door and glance down the hall to the entrance where I met Bernie earlier today. I should go down and pack up some of those Morgan Sidney costumes, but the idea of stepping out that door makes me nervous. I swallow hard a couple of times to ease my suddenly dry mouth. The last time I walked through that door, it got very spooky when I came back here. I guess the costumes can wait.

I ease down onto my satin stool in front of my movie star mirror. Okay, okay, all that spooky crap sounds ridiculous. I'm being silly. The crew was on a break, that's all. Or everyone had to go to another stage to help move sets or furniture really quickly to squeeze in one last scene of the day. Happens all the time. Just nobody told me about it.

And yes, sometimes it feels like it's 1935 in here, but that's because everything on this set is on a more human scale. No Titanic icebergs, no interplanetary spaceships, no slobbery monsters, no ray guns, no super powers, none of that stuff. It's all very adult, and I like that.

At least, in those days, *people* still mattered; human feelings and human sympathy could still draw an audience.

Actors and actresses don't count anymore. It's all about the big picture, a bunch of glittering generalities. We're all just unimportant little nobodies who don't count.

And Hadley Finch-Scott, phooey on you and your cross country car chase with lots of action. I don't even like to *watch* movies like that. Why would I want to help make one?

But I'm being silly. Those days are long gone. And the fun, innocent, and wise films they made in those days are as gone as the Americans who made them.

In my cute little stripped chiffon suit, I look at myself in the movie star mirror, and I'm tearing up a little, mostly in self pity. Working here today hasn't been a complete waste of my time by any means. I've met all these great people. And apparently we're back tomorrow for more of the same. Of course, these pictures won't do a thing for my career, other than bury it and me with it. And zilch at the box office, if they ever even get there. These are probably some of those straight to video deals that three people watch at 4 am on cable somewhere. I mean, nobody working here is anybody I've ever heard of, for Pete's sake.

But so what? I've met Alan. Why does even the thought of that guy take my breath away? Make me feel stupidly happy? Make my heart dance the rumba? Because I like him. A lot. How often does *that* happen? How about never, in my case. We've certainly got some chemistry and maybe even something more. That would be a first for me.

I really admire the guy, slogging along here in this thankless junk heap of shattered dreams called show biz, unrewarded, unnoticed and unlikely to ever get anywhere. As an actor, Alan really has something special, in my opinion, a kind of integrity. Okay, I'll say it, a kind of laughter and intelligence in the eyes, mixed with sweetness and light. Corny, yes, but real. But good luck pal, nobody wants *that* anymore. As the saying goes, talent and $2.25 will get you a ride on the subway.

I look at the pile of my street clothes, faded torn jeans and a couple of chic strappy tee shirts all of which cost me a bundle at one of Beverly Hills' for-Hollywood-suckers, rip off boutiques, and which basically look like rags. Wow, how depressing! What do I think of myself? Sure, they're trendy and comfortable, but this dress is comfortable, too, and lots more fun to wear and look at. I'm keeping it on. I'll never charm a guy like Alan in those other duds. With one last look in the mirror to fluff my hair, apply some color to the lips and puff the face with pale white Gardenia powder, I'm ready to conquer the world and my Captain as I head for the green room.

He's standing there, sort of waiting for me, I think.

"It was fun today," I say. Why not flatter his ego a little? He won't get much flattery anywhere else in Hollywood. "You're a really good actor."

He smiles, pleased.

"I mean that."

"Well thanks. Coming from you that's quite a compliment. I had fun today, too. You're hot stuff, baby," he smiles and waits.

"Thanks." Hot stuff? He's gotta be talking about that last kiss. "Well," I titter in embarrassment, "I'm not always so hot...No wait, what I mean is that kiss wasn't acting, not for me."

He smiles, his eyes are like pale blue pools of mischief and desire. He moves closer, puts his arms around me, and in a low, tremulous voice, confesses, "me either."

We're at it again, kissing for real. And I lose track of time, and where I am, and everything. When we pause for a breath, he says;

"Would you like to go out to dinner with me tonight?"

"I'd love it." I take a deep breath to more or less regain consciousness. I've gotta give him the standard show biz boilerplate disclaimer. "But I want to be right up front about everything. If you're thinking I can help your career, don't get your hopes up, because I can't even help my own career. As a matter of fact, my agent told me to retire only this morning. Okay? I wish I *could* do something for you. You seem very talented to me. But believe me the huddled masses suck when it comes to taste, and the boys in the big offices are just as infantile. It's a hopeless world. But what do we care? Fuck it. Let's just screw it all and go to Peoria and open a chili joint or something."

He gazes into my eyes. "Let's just forget all that." He draws me tightly into his protective embrace, kisses me so gently, so passionately, I do forget it all.

"Feeling better?" he asks. I nod. Better doesn't even begin to describe how I feel. "Good," he says. "For the moment, our lucky stars are in alignment. The huddled masses are on our side, and big boys in the offices love making money, so it's happy days for us. Now, I'm having them bring my Duesy around to the stage door. You look swell, so if you're ready, I can't keep my fans waiting too long."

I've got that spooky feeling all over again. Chills down the spine. This isn't adding up right. "Your fans? Your Duesy? As in Duesenberg? Do you drive an antique Duesenberg? Wait a minute, are we involved in some sort of cult film thing? Is that what this is?"

"Oh, stop worrying about the business. What do you say, let's go dancing at the Cocoanut Grove, and really shake this town up, give the fans and gossip columnists something to talk about?"

Holy Shit! *What's going on here?* The Cocoanut Grove was demolished along with the Ambassador Hotel *years* ago. But in the nineteen thirties it was *the* place to see and be seen. This can't be happening. I finally meet a guy I can't live without, and he's not even from my century. It can't be, but that has to be what's going on here. There's no other way any of this makes sense. I walked out of the past into my present when I met Bernie. And it was hard to come back. I think I almost didn't make it. But, to really go back to the nineteen thirties, to leave everything I know for a world that's very, very different and very, very scary. I don't know if I can do that, or if I even want to do that.

Alan is looking at me expectantly. I want to just bury myself in his chest and forget about everything else. But nineteen thirty!!! This is too, too spooky. I'm hyperventilating.

"The Cocoanut Grove?" I pant, totally stupefied, staring at him and wondering if I've seen him on Turner Classic movies. I need some time to think. "Sure, sounds great. But I left my hand bag in my dressing room. I'll be right back."

"I'll be waiting right here, baby. Don't be long."

I dash through the green room back to my dressing room and collapse on my satin cushion, shaking so hard I can hardly light my cigarette. Now I'm officially in shock.

It's got to be, OMG, the nineteen thirties!!! I wish I'd paid more attention in my history classes. Didn't the stock market crash in '29? Didn't the Great Depression come next, and last for like ten horrible years? And then World War II in the early nineteen forties? Whoa! I'm wouldn't exactly going back to the Garden of Eden, would I?

No TV? No internet? I don' think they even had antibiotics. No cell phones? Did they have Novocain for when your teeth get drilled by the dentist?

Oh Shit! If I start thinking of all the things they didn't have in the nineteen thirties, I'll chicken out. I won't be able to do this. And I'll lose the first guy I've ever met who makes me believe love and romance aren't a joke. And he has a Duesenberg. He must be a movie star of some magnitude to have a Duesy. So the movies we did today must do pretty good at the box office. He said the huddled masses are on our side. I won't end up in Peoria. That is, unless I go back to my present.

But I'm practically paralyzed with terror. I get up and slowly walk to the exit door and wrap my hand around the knob to keep from panicking. I can get back to my century, if I need to. I really don't think I can stay here. I just can't. It's way too scary. My sweaty hand slides over the slippery, metal knob, as I start to turn it.

Breathlessly, I try to think. I'm pretty sure, from my last experience meeting Bernie out front, that if I go out the hall door, I'm back in my twenty-first century world, a world that has absolutely no use for me. On the other hand—deep drags of my low tar cigarette are making me so dizzy I can't think straight—if I go back through the green room to Alan, I have a great boyfriend, screaming fans and a great career waiting for me. And I'm doing work that I'm very proud of, that's very popular with audiences, and that is a real hoot to be involved in.

Then I remember what Alan said about why these movies are big box office. They make you believe that even if all you have is gumption, humor and generosity, you can make it. Well, right about now, for the first time in my life, I'd line up around the block for a big dose of that.

If I go out this door, my best and only hope is that Finch-Scott thinks I'll look great in some skimpy little halter top behind the wheel of a convertible for the world's longest car chase picture. I'll go back to my bland, modern life, where I don't get to be 'the girl', don't get 'the guy', no great costumes, I don't even have a job or a boyfriend, and there aren't any jobs or boyfriends that I want. Jeeze, what happened to the movies?

There's a tap on my dressing room door, and I hear Alan ask, "can I come in?"

Still clinging to my doorknob, I turn to face the opposite door. "Sure, come in."

He enters, almost shyly. "I came to see what was taking so long. I know I was awfully hard on you today. I hope you can forgive me."

"No, no, I learned a lot. I really like these pictures we're doing. Even when I thought they were losers and that we'd end up slinging hash in Peoria, I was proud of my work and glad that at least I'd tried to do something good."

He gives me a puzzled glance, because I'm rambling between two centuries. With a bemused smile, he asks, "What have you got against Peoria?"

"Oh, nothing, nothing at all. Don't mind me. (I take the last drag on the ciggie, and stub it out) And, anyway, I think it was me that was tough on you. But you're such a big, good looking, masculine guy, you seemed to have an unfair advantage. You're such a real guy's guy, that I'm sure men admire you. And Iris says women fall for you like ninepins in a bowling alley. I wasn't about to be another ninepin."

"You? Another ninepin? Don't make me laugh. Just promise me one thing, stop making fun of me about how you're going to help my career. Yes, I'm such a big star now, it's embarrassing. But it was a long hard road to get here."

"Oh!" I'd forgotten that in my arrogant past, or actually back in my arrogant present, I thought I was the big star, and he was the nobody. "I'm sorry. I was just teasing."

I'm still clinging to the door knob, my escape hatch to the twenty first century. I might be able to do a 'run, Nicky, run' on a movie set, but my courage is failing me here. I look down, bite my lip, and sigh.

Alan just stands there, staring at me. Finally he says, "Look, if you don't want to come, I'll understand. For all the hoopla they print about me in the papers, I'm nothing very special. Just a lucky guy."

I look up. I was just lucky, too. I could like this guy, even if his kisses didn't buckle my knees. Then our eyes meet, and if a thousand centuries separated us, I'd never forget those eyes or the look he gives me.

"But," he says bashfully, "I really want to go out with you because I'm in already in love with you. In case you haven't guessed, that was me last week at the Grove who had the band play the Wedding March twice, each time you entered the club. That's why I was standing there waiting for you. But you were laughing so hard with your friends, you didn't even notice me. You have a great laugh. I love hearing it."

My mouth falls open in shock. I guess I've been laughing my way out of trouble for a century. "You played the Wedding March *twice* for me?"

He blushes. I can't believe I've made him blush.

"I meant it as a joke. But when I saw you there with the Wedding March playing, I knew the joke was on me. I knew that I was crazy about you and wanted that music to be playing for us for real."

He moves toward me and kisses me lightly. My heart seems to fly up into my throat, but my hand is still clinging to the doorknob.

"I'm in love with you. Do you think you could ever feel anything for me?"

His voice, that dulcet baritone resonating effortlessly in his powerful chest, almost brings tears to my eyes. He's so close to me that he feels like part of me. I could never leave him. This is where the sneering scorner exits stage left. Goodbye cynical me, hello beautiful dreamer. Am I gonna throw away the whole twenty first century for a guy I've known only a couple of hours? Ever hear of love at first sight? I feel that malaria coming on again, that ache to believe, that elemental force that makes us reach for joy. Yes, I want to have a great love story. I want to be part of great movies. I'm scared to death, but I'm too excited to worry about it.

"Yeah, I think maybe I could. Let's go. I'm dying for a ride in that Duesy."

Alan takes me by the hand, and we head for the studio exit. All I can think is that he played the Wedding March twice for me and was too embarrassed to admit it. What guy! He smiles that great smile of his, a smile worth jumping over the moon for.

When we get to the exit door, he puts his arm protectively around my shoulders and pulls me close.

"Are you ready, baby? When they see us together, they'll go wild."

The door opens and we step out. Studio guards with linked arms are holding the surging crowds back. The roar that greets us is deafening. Flashbulbs explode like fireworks lighting up the evening sky. He squeezes me to him and gives me the biggest grin I've ever seen, a grin that pierces my heart like nothing ever before. Never in my wildest dreams...

ABOUT THE AUTHOR

Marcy Casterline O'Rourke worked extensively in the fashion industry as a model with Eileen Ford, while attending Barnard College. She also studied acting and worked in television, film, and theater and married actor/screenwriter Tom O'Rourke, who went on to play "Justin" on The Guiding Light. After working in the soap world for seven years, they moved to LA for 10 years where Tom continued to pursue acting on many night time series (see imdb.com for complete list) and their son Preston was born. Moving back to the New York area, Tom became a regular on Law & Order, and Marcy settled into motherhood and various sales jobs to make ends meet. With the blessing of her husband, she turned to writing as an outlet for her creative energies. A ROGUE, A PIRATE AND A DRY MARTINI is her second novel.

Made in the USA
Monee, IL
20 December 2021